W9-BKU-261

MAKING IT

BARBARA
CORCORAN

MAKING IT

AN ATLANTIC MONTHLY PRESS BOOK
Little, Brown and Company
BOSTON   TORONTO

FIRST EDITION

For lines from "Others, I am not the first," by A. E. Housman, acknowledgment is made to The Society of Authors as the literary representative of the Estate of A. E. Housman, and Jonathan Cape, Ltd., publishers of A. E. Housman's *Collected Poems*. From *A Shropshire Lad*, Authorised Edition, from *The Collected Poems of A. E. Housman*. Copyright 1939, 1940, © 1965 by Holt, Rinehart and Winston. Copyright © 1967, 1968 by Robert E. Symons. Reprinted by permission of Holt, Rinehart and Winston, Publishers.

Library of Congress Cataloging in Publication Data

Corcoran, Barbara.
    Making it.

    "An Atlantic Monthly Press book."
    SUMMARY: Just as she begins to take charge of her life, the 17-year-old daughter of a small-town minister is forced to face the truth about the sister she idolizes.
    [1. Brothers and sisters—Fiction] I. Title.
PZ7.C814Ma   [Fic]   80-24769
ISBN 0-316-15731-7

ATLANTIC–LITTLE, BROWN BOOKS
ARE PUBLISHED BY
LITTLE, BROWN AND COMPANY
IN ASSOCIATION WITH
THE ATLANTIC MONTHLY PRESS

BP

Published simultaneously in Canada
by Little, Brown & Company (Canada) Limited

PRINTED IN THE UNITED STATES OF AMERICA

For Andrea Dixon,
whose help and encouragement
I couldn't have done without

MAKING IT

1 ❁ ❁

CHARLOTTE was coming home. I could hardly believe it, but my mom handed me the letter and that was what it said all right. "Dear Mom: Surprise, surprise, your favorite daughter is coming home for Easter. Dying to see you all. Love, Charlotte."

We hadn't seen her since she went back to college after Christmas a year ago. She hadn't even written much for the last six or eight months, not even to me, and I'm her favorite.

I was so happy, I leaned over and kissed my brother Harvey on the forehead, and he scrunched back in his wheelchair and grinned up at me. Harvey is the youngest of the six of us, and he is retarded, but I love him, except when he throws one of his temper tantrums, which are scary. My mother builds her whole life around Harvey now that Charlotte is gone, and I wondered how it would be for her, getting used to Charlotte again, even temporarily.

Charlotte is the beautiful one, the sparkly one, the gifted one. My three oldest sisters, all married and away, are nice but nothing spectacular. My twin, Robert, died when we were eight, and since then I have always felt like a shadow around the house. Charlotte and Harvey are the outstanding ones.

My mother isn't much for expressing extravagant feel-

3

ings, but I could see she was excited when we came out of the post office. We walked right past Olsen's drugstore before she remembered Harvey's prescription. I ran to get it, and when I came back, Mrs. Walford had descended upon my mom. Mrs. Walford is excruciatingly boring and sometimes downright mean, but when your father is a minister in a small Colorado town, you're supposed to be tolerant of people — at least that's what I was brought up to believe.

Harvey had turned on his transistor. I think it's his way of tuning out people he doesn't like. When Mrs. Walford peered at him in her nearsighted nosy way, he turned up the volume. Some violinist was playing a Haydn concerto, and the music spun out like a golden thread, and for a minute both Harvey and I forgot Mrs. Walford. Then she nudged my arm and said, "You must be real excited about Charlotte coming. You and she were always such pals."

I said yes, I was excited, and yes I would be glad to see her, and yes I had missed her, and yes I would be graduating from high in June. I tried not to sound rude, but it wasn't easy. Luckily Mrs. Walford, like everyone else, pays very little attention to what I say or don't say.

Pretty soon she shuffled off, and we went down the main street of our town, Fort Lewis, which hasn't grown much since it began in 1902. It's in the eastern part of the state, where the wind blows a lot. The people are mostly farmers and ranchers, and one of their favorite hobbies is keeping up with other people's business. Charlotte despised them. I tried to put them out of my mind. I have enough to think about, keeping up my grade level. I was going to need all the scholarship and aid money I could get. My father's church was dirt-poor, and his salary was often, as he liked to say "more honored in the breach than in the observance." (If that's how the quotation goes; he says I misquote everything.)

We usually had enough food and clothes, because everybody dumped their castoffs and leftovers on us. That's the

Christian practice. We were supposed to be grateful, but my most burning ambition was to go into a store and buy a whole wardrobe that was my own. The way Charlotte did when she went to college. My mother did some fancy wheeling and dealing to get Charlotte into the college of her choice, Smith, where she was now in her second year.

Mom got her a scholarship and a federal loan and then from somewhere, maybe the savings account she was always so mysterious about, she found the money for Charlotte's new clothes. I knew Mom would never go through all that for me. I'd have to get there under my own steam. I'd already parted with twenty dollars apiece in filing fees at UCLA and the University of Denver, and when I was accepted and made up my mind which one I was going to, it would be another fifty dollars for my Statement of Intention. Nonrefundable. It would probably be Denver, though that was not my preference. I wanted to get far away from Colorado. No matter how I figured it, though, the cost of living in Los Angeles was just beyond me. Unless a miracle occurred.

As soon as we turned into our yard, Harvey hauled himself out of the wheelchair. He hates the chair. He'd rather walk but he walks in such a slow, dingtoed way, sometimes falling over his own feet, that Mom gets embarrassed when people notice him. She seems to think the wheelchair is more acceptable.

Daddy was home, for a change, and when Mom told him that Charlotte was coming, I was shocked at how dismayed he looked. He always had bragged about Charlotte, how pretty she was and how smart. I really used to mind because he never praised me. He was kind to me the way somebody is to the old family dog, somebody who isn't crazy about dogs. But I guess when Charlotte went away, he felt she had been wiped out of his life. If she was coming back, he would have to brace himself for a resurrection.

He spends most of his time in his little study at the

church. He says he has to be accessible. And people do come to see him a lot. Sometimes they come from somewhere else and stay long enough to make my mother look pretty grim. She always blamed Mr. Johnson, one of Daddy's old seminary buddies, for Robert's getting diphtheria. Hardly anybody gets diphtheria any more, unless they've caught it from somebody traveling in strange places, and Mr. Johnson, who was a missionary, had definitely been traveling in strange places. Mom was sure he was a carrier of diphtheria, because nobody could account any other way for Robert's catching it. Dr. Means thought it was tonsillitis, until it was too late to cure him.

My father never admitted that Mr. Johnson might have caused Robert's death, but I know he thought about it a lot. Also, to add to his guilt, my father had whipped Robert just a few days before he got sick, for something Robert hadn't done. I think Daddy saw Robert's death as a punishment from God. After that he held himself aloof from the family, refusing to make decisions or get involved in our affairs. It was like having a ghost father.

My mother was also on a guilt trip because when Robert and I were little, she had refused to let us get any kind of shots or immunizations. She was going through a "nature will take care of them" kick. There was a fuss at the school, but I guess because she was the minister's wife and a determined woman, she got away with it. Dr. Means said he would be alive today if he had had his shots. Afterward Harvey and I got all the shots going, a good example of locking the barn door. Even I felt guilty, because I was still alive and my twin was dead. Robert left us a heavy heritage.

So my father turned into a man that none of us could depend on for anything except the occasional dollop of Biblical advice. I suppose he figured he couldn't go wrong if he stuck with the word of God. With his parishioners he was one hundred percent sympathy and understanding, but

6

if we wanted anything from him, whether it was putting on the storm windows or easing a breaking heart, he slipped away. He became for me the shadow of an illusion, like the bunny ears you make on the wall when you're trying to get to sleep.

Now, speaking of Charlotte, he said, "It's very expensive, coming all this way for Easter."

"She didn't ask us for the money," my mother said. "Charlotte hasn't asked us for a cent since Christmas, Raymond."

"She'll have big ideas," he said. "Wanting breakfast in bed and all that fancy eastern stuff."

My mother, who is from upstate New York, laughed. "What makes you think easterners have breakfast in bed?"

He didn't argue. He went off to the church, eating one of the bananas my mother had bought for Harvey. I watched him hurry down the path, his shoulders hunched against the wind, although for once there wasn't any. I suspect he hated being surrounded by women. Robert had been his link with some real place where he could hold up his head and be proud, and now that was gone.

Soon after Robert's death my mother had to talk to my father about Harvey not being right in the head. He must have begun to realize it, but I suppose he didn't want to face it. Harvey was only two years old then, and it's easy to kid yourself if you want to badly enough. You can say, "He's a little slower than the others," and "He'll catch up," stuff like that. But of course Mom knew.

Harvey doesn't look especially retarded, if you don't talk to him. He's not a Mongoloid type or anything. In some ways he seems almost normal. For instance, he loves music, and he knows the names of a lot of composers and pieces of music, more than I do, in fact. But most of the time he acts more like a little kid, and he has trouble speaking words clearly.

7

It has been very hard on my mother, and she has devoted herself to him. He adores Charlotte, as we all do, but my older sisters left home before he was very old, so they don't really feel comfortable with him. He is a very lovable boy, actually, full of affection. And when he heard Charlotte was coming home, he hugged himself and rocked back and forth in his chair saying, "Charla, Charla," until my mother kissed him and said, "All right, Harvey, all right now."

All of us felt a little giddy because Charlotte was coming.

2 ❁ ❁

SHE never said what day she would arrive. Every afternoon I rushed home after school to check before I went down to the Aspen View Cafe, where I wash dishes. My mother cleaned up the house about five times, and baked Charlotte's favorite layer cake three times. Each time, we had to eat it up before it got too stale, no hardship for the rest of us. My father kept saying Charlotte wouldn't come at all, but he is always afraid of hoping. I had everything ready so I could move all my clothes to the hall closet when she came. Charlotte and I always shared a room. I'd have moved out altogether and slept on the sofa, but Mom got pretty sharp about that.

"It's your sister that's coming," she said, "not the Empress Eugenie."

Still, I did everything I could to make it Charlotte's room. I took down all my posters and stowed them in the closet, and I emptied three of the four bureau drawers and gave myself the one that sticks. I remembered how mad Charlotte used to get at that drawer. You can see the marks where she would kick it.

I Windexed the mirror and I put her books on the top shelves of the bookcase. *Wuthering Heights, Jane Eyre, Rebecca, Jamaica Inn, Gone With the Wind,* a biography of Vivien Leigh, and *Judy,* about Judy Garland: those had

9

been her favorites that she read over and over. I got a Coke bottle that she had painted flowers on when she was in the eighth grade, and I filled it with pussywillows.

But she didn't come and she didn't come. It got to be Maundy Thursday, and then Good Friday. On Saturdays I worked all day at the cafe, but I was on needles and pins every time a car went by. The last time she had come to Denver by bus, and hitchhiked to Fort Lewis. My parents were appalled, and when it was time for her to go, Daddy drove her to Denver, complaining all the way. He hates traffic.

It got to be five-thirty and she hadn't come. I thought of Harvey's eager look every time the front door opened and how he would say, "Charla?" and for a moment I felt annoyed with my sister for keeping everyone on edge this way. But that was Charlotte; she never really understood how much what she did affected us. She couldn't believe it mattered to anyone but herself. And if you loved her, you had to take her as she was. And I did love her, more than anyone. She was my ideal.

At six I finished work and started to walk home. I was tired. I felt as if I had washed a million glasses and cups and plates, and an ocean of forks and knives and spoons. People eat too much and drink too much coffee. My father says gluttony is a sin. If you don't believe it, he says, look it up. He means in the Bible.

When I was nearly home, a car pulled up alongside me, and I was almost too tired to look, but it might be somebody I knew, and if I didn't speak, they'd say I was getting high hat. So I stopped. The sun was in my eyes and I couldn't see the driver, but the car was a new Mustang. The person in the driver's seat got out and shouted, "Sissy!" and I nearly fell over. It was Charlotte, looking like something out of *Harper's Bazaar*. She ran to me and swung me off my feet, and kissed me and hugged me, and she smelled

10

marvelous. She was wearing a high-crowned hat that looked terrific. She's just barely twenty-one, but she looked as sophisticated as a movie star.

The rest of that evening is a blur of happiness in my mind. Charlotte came like a fresh breeze that picked us up and whirled us around until we were giddy. Even my dad was smiling all over his face, and he postponed an appointment he had. Mom somehow produced another one of those cakes, and we had Charlotte's favorite chili that my mother makes better than anybody.

All I can remember about myself is that I sat and listened and glowed inside. I was so proud of my sister, I could have burst. She was always glamorous, even when she was a kid, but something new had been added. She seemed awfully grownup, and I was almost scared of her. She looked beautiful in a pale green pantsuit that brought out the green flecks in her eyes, and when she took off her hat, her hair looked as if it had just been done by somebody famous on Fifth Avenue or in Beverly Hills, although she had flown in all the way from Boston.

My mom is not a demonstrative lady, but she kept scrubbing at her eyes as if to keep from crying. She asked a lot of questions, as she always does. Like where did Charlotte get that Mustang?

"I rented it at the airport." She smiled and gave Mom a hug. "I remembered what a hullabaloo you and Dad raised when I hitchhiked last year." She lit a cigarette.

"You've taken up smoking," Daddy said, frowning.

"I've taken up honesty," she said. "I've smoked for years, Dad. I was always scared to let you know."

"You'll get cancer," my mother said.

"I don't think so. Remember, Dad always said, 'Nothing happens to Charlotte.' 'The wages of sin pass you by,' you used to say, Dad, and you couldn't understand it. Remember?"

11

"I remember."

"Once when you were really provoked with me, you preached a sermon about actions and consequences."

My mother said, "Nobody is exempt from consequences."

Charlotte got up and brought the coffee pot into the living room. "Daddy said I lived a charmed life."

"I remember his saying that." It was the first remark I had made since we finished dinner. "He was mad because you got A's without doing your homework."

My mother settled back in her favorite rocker and got out her knitting. "Well, now, supposing you tell us all about your charmed life. I know you wrote you had a job after classes and weekends, but that's an expensive suit. And what about that car?"

"Oh, I'll turn the car back in a day or two. Maybe Sissy will drive me over to Fort Collins or wherever the nearest rental agency is. You've got your license now, haven't you, Sis?"

"Yes." I looked at my father. He almost never lets me have the car.

"Good. Then some day when Dad isn't using the car."

"You haven't mentioned college," my mother said, "and you write so seldom, I feel out of touch."

There was a pause while Charlotte ground out her cigarette and poured some more coffee. "Mother, I'm not in college any more. I left right after Christmas break."

The only sound in the room was Harvey coughing and clearing his throat, the way he does all the time. He turned his transistor up, and there was a sudden blare of hard rock.

My father said, "Turn that thing off."

Harvey whimpered a little and turned it down low.

My mother was looking very pale. I knew she must be thinking of all the letters she had written, all the long-distance calls she had made, and the forms she labored over, to get Charlotte into college in the first place. She had set

12

so much store by Charlotte, maybe expecting of her the things she would have liked to do herself. But all she said was, "Perhaps you had better explain."

Charlotte leaned forward and touched Mom's wrist, her face serious, almost pleading. "Please understand. I couldn't take it any longer, truly."

"Take what?"

"College. Maybe I'm weird or something, but honestly, all that energy spent impressing people, going out with X number of boys to prove you're popular, even if they're the most boring creeps in the country. And being left out of things because I'm some hick from out West, having my clothes looked at as if they were rags . . ."

Something was wrong. I adored my sister, but I knew when she was inventing a story. It seemed to me that something had made her quit college that she couldn't talk to our parents about, so she was making something up. This was the middle of her second year, after all. My father accepted it at once, and gave a short sermon on vanity that nobody listened to. My mother's dark eyes searched Charlotte's face. She didn't buy the story either, I could tell. But I think Mom learned years ago that you couldn't bully the truth out of Charlotte. Charlotte guarded her privacy more fiercely than anyone I had ever known.

But Charlotte was aware of Mom's scrutiny and it was making her nervous. "My roommate," she said, "I had a roommate this year that really drove me up the wall. I don't think I'm all that hard to live with . . . am I, Sissy?" She went on before I could do more than shake my head. She *isn't* hard to live with, not at all. "My roommate got up with the birds. For what seemed like hours she would brush her teeth and gargle and make nauseating noises. Then she'd say, 'Rise and shine, Charlotte. It's the first day of the rest of your life.'" Charlotte laughed, and looked at Mom appealingly. "I couldn't stand it."

13

"I suppose you could have changed your roommate," Mom said.

"I couldn't do that. It would have been a real trauma for her, to be rejected like that."

I believed her about the roommate. Charlotte always hated to hurt people, even when she was little. Sometimes she'd make up the biggest stories you ever heard just to keep from saying something unpleasant or hurtful to someone. Like when she got elected captain of the softball team just when she'd decided not to go out for it anymore because she wanted to go bike riding with Jerry Newcombe. She told everybody she'd torn the cartilage in her knee, and she was so convincing, Betty Haggarty sent her some flowers. Charlotte had to limp for a long time after that.

My mother put down her knitting. 'If you aren't in college, just what are you doing? It would have been nice, I think, if you'd let us know."

"Mom, I'm sorry. I hated to tell you because I knew you'd be upset."

"You lack moral courage, Charlotte," my father said.

"You're absolutely right, I do. I know I do."

"What are you doing?" My mother hates to let conversations get off the track. "Where are you living?"

Charlotte lighted another cigarette. I noticed they were a kind that's low in tar. "I was so lucky. I have this marvelous job. Kind of a spin-off of the one I had last summer."

"What kind of job?"

"I'm a glorified secretary. I have a lot of responsibility really, and it's very interesting."

"What kind of business?"

"Well, it's sort of a consulting firm. I get to travel sometimes even. That's why I could come home for Easter."

My mother studied her. "I can't think of anyone in Fort Lewis anybody would care to consult."

Charlotte laughed. "I didn't mean I'm *here* on business. I'll be going to the coast."

14

"What coast?" my father said.

"West coast. Los Angeles."

"Hollywood?" my mother said.

"Not especially Hollywood. Just Los Angeles."

My dad looked at his watch. "I ought to check in at the church," he said. "Henderson forgets to lock up sometimes."

"Sit still, Raymond," my mother said. And to Charlotte: "How long will you be with us, then?"

"I'm not sure. I have to wait for a phone call. From my boss." She glanced at me. "If a call comes when I'm not here, would whoever answers be an angel and get the number I'm to call? It's very important."

I said, "Sure." I was worried about what she was telling us. I was sure there was more to it.

Charlotte looked at Mom. She had her head bent, so her hair fell forward around her face, making her look really beautiful. "Mom," she said, "I guess I like to make my own way. That was part of the trouble with college — I still felt like some little school kid. I'm like you, I have to be independent."

It was the right thing to say. My mother prides herself on her independence. She relaxed a little and said, "I won't pretend it isn't a terrible disappointment. We set such store by you."

"Can't you still? It doesn't mean I died or something, just because I dropped out of college." She gave a nervous little laugh. "Lots of famous people dropped out."

"Einstein," my father said.

"Mom, I mean to make something of my life. I mean to live well and hold my head up and never..." she spread her hands out in an appeal to my mother "...never wear hand-me-down clothes again, never have to apologize for being me, never be scared of stupid people."

My mother looked past all of us, staring at the dark windowpanes, and I wondered what she was thinking.

"If you have virtue and goodness, you are armed against the world," my father said.

My mother sighed.

Harvey turned up his radio again and said, "Charla? Charla?"

She jumped up and went over to his chair. "I brought you some albums, Harvey. Beethoven's First Piano Concerto."

He beamed up at her. "I like him."

"I know you do." She gave him a quick hug. "Sissy, come on upstairs and help me unpack, okay? Whose room do I have?"

"You're still in with me." I felt apologetic. My beautiful sister with her beautiful clothes. "Mom gave the girls' beds to the O'Briens when their house burned down."

"That's wonderful," Charlotte said. "We can talk all night."

I heard what my mom said as we were leaving the room. She spoke so low, to herself, I don't think anyone else heard her. "Charlotte's gone," she said.

3 ✲ ✲

ASTER Sunday was a happy day. Although I was sure she didn't want to, Charlotte went to church with us, and it was really great to hear her singing those Alleluia hymns. Easter is my favorite church day, it's so full of hope. Charlotte has a beautiful singing voice, low and really thrilling. In high school she sang with the school chorus, and her senior year she sang with Georgie Bullock's combo at school dances.

People greeted her warmly after church, and even Mrs. Walford managed to be civil, though I could see all the questions in her eyes. Charlotte was gracious to all of them, and she looked terrific. Even Daddy's sermon was good. He almost sounded the way I remember him, when I was little, authoritative and convincing.

About as soon as we got home from church, the phone started ringing, and pretty soon all of Charlotte's old buddies who were still around started coming, both male and female. Mom complained that she couldn't ever get the car backed out of the yard, but I could see she was pleased that Charlotte was still such a big hit.

For the next week or so, I hardly saw my sister. Mom began to get antsy about Charlotte's late hours, and she didn't listen when I said after all Charlotte was grown up. When I said it again, a day or two later, she said, "She is living under our roof. Your father is a minister in this town. It matters what you children do."

I knew she was hurt and disappointed. But, I mean, "you children"? Actually I wondered myself what Charlotte was doing. Sometimes when she came home, she reeked of whiskey, and other times I could smell pot. I'm sure Mom could smell it too; she never went to sleep till after Charlotte got home, although she didn't come out to speak to her. I'd see her light go out after ours did.

Sometimes Charlotte would sit up in bed with her arms around her knees and talk about the evening, but other times she just said, "Hi, go to sleep," and went straight to bed. I knew she was going out a lot with Don McClaren, who used to date her in high school. She'd been in love with his older brother once. She told me they sometimes drove over to a town about twenty miles away where Georgie Bullock owned a bar. He had a new group now, but they played late at night and when Charlotte went there, Georgie asked her to sing. I would have loved to hear her, but she would never ask me along on a double date. She began to go there quite a lot, sometimes with Don and sometimes by herself. She still had the Mustang, which worried my father no end. He kept figuring up what it must be costing her. Finally she told him she had paid a month's rent on it, and would he please quit fussing about it.

During the day I guess she slept till noon or after. She was always up and usually gone when I got home, but Mom did a lot of griping about her sleeping in. Sleep always seems to have struck my mother as being slightly sinful.

Late one afternoon, about ten days after Charlotte had come home, I got to the house just in time for a first-class row. At first I couldn't figure out what had happened. Harvey was weaving up and down the hall looking spacy and giggling, and my mother and Charlotte were yelling at each other. Well, it turned out that Charlotte had given

18

Harvey a few drags on a marijuana cigarette, and my mother was beside herself.

"It's bad enough you acting the way you do," she yelled, "coming in all hours smelling of whiskey and dope, without corrupting your poor helpless brother."

"I was only trying to give him a little pleasure," Charlotte said. "God knows he has little enough."

"Look at him," Mom said. "He's out of his senses."

"What better place could he be?"

"You are a wicked girl, corrupting your brother."

One reason they had to raise their voices was that the stereo was on, playing a Billie Holiday album. Mom pointed toward our room, were the stereo was, and said, "Shut that thing off."

"I like it," Charlotte said.

My mother turned to me. "Go shut that off."

"Leave it alone," Charlotte said.

I didn't know what to do, so I just stood there, feeling sick to my stomach, while they glared at each other. Mom marched into the room and turned off the stereo.

"That was Billie Holiday," Charlotte said. "That happens to be my favorite record. In case you don't know, she was a . . ."

Mom cut in. "I know who Billie Holiday was. She killed herself with dope."

Charlotte's expression changed. She smiled a strange little smile, and her voice when she spoke was softer. "Hey, Mother, when you lived back there in the Hudson Valley, did you used to go down to New York and cut loose now and then? Did you ever hear Billie Holiday?"

"I'm not that old, thank you," Mom snapped.

Charlotte laughed. "Mom, don't come on all dewy-eyed innocence with me." She paused, watching Mom's face. "I had a nice visit with Aunt Pearl. Did I write you about my nice visit?"

19

Mom caught her breath. "You didn't write me about it, no."

Something was happening in my mother's face that I couldn't read.

"We had a dandy time. Aunt Pearl got out all the old family albums, and told me all the dirt about everybody." She waited again, as if she expected some answer. "You were quite a family."

They stared hard at each other for such a long time, I began to feel scared. It was as if something dangerous had just been said. Finally Mom walked away and looked out the hall window, which you can't see out of because it's diamond-paned and tinted yellow.

"How long will you be with us?" Mom's voice was entirely different, as if she were speaking to a casual visitor.

"I'm moving out in the morning," Charlotte said, in a matching polite voice. "I have to stay in town till I hear from Jerry, but I'll be at the Highlander Motel. I'd appreciate it if you'd give him that number when he calls."

"Fine," my mother said.

Charlotte went into our room and closed the door. Harvey waved to me and stumbled into his room. I knew I should go look after him but I couldn't seem to move. Mom still stood at the window, back to me. Her shoulders shook and I knew she was crying.

4 ❀ ❀

AFTER Charlotte moved into the motel, Mom never spoke her name. It was just as if Charlotte had never come back at all. Once in a while Daddy made a plaintive remark about never seeing her, or just seeing her drive by "in that expensive car," but my mother would make no answer at all. Harvey cried for her.

With school and my job and my homework I didn't have much spare time, but I did ride my bike out to the highway, where the motel was. If it was before four or five in the afternoon, Charlotte would still be asleep, but if she heard my knock she'd let me in, and she always seemed glad to see me.

I was afraid she wasn't eating much, not because she didn't have the money, but because she always did neglect things like food, so I began to bring stuff that would be good for her, like oranges and bananas, fresh bread, and vitamin pills. She seemed touched, and sometimes she would hug me and say nobody really cared about her but me. It was a new side of her that I hadn't seen; I had usually thought of her as absolutely sure of herself and invulnerable. It hurt to see her feeling down.

One day she said, "I'm not going to ask you again about phone calls. He's not going to call. He's ditched me."

"Why should your boss ditch you?"

She was on the bed, her arms wrapped around her knees, looking moody. "He wasn't really my boss. He managed the club where I worked, but I was responsible to the band."

"I thought you worked for a consulting company."

"That was for Mom's benefit. Imagine her reaction if I said I was singing in a second-rate club."

"You're breaking her heart, Charlotte. I wish you'd come see her sometimes."

"She wouldn't approve of my life-style." She laughed. "Which is really funny. You know what Aunt Pearl told me?"

"How should I know what Aunt Pearl told you?" I had a feeling I didn't want to know.

"When Mom was about your age, she had an abortion." I stared at her. "I don't believe it."

She shrugged. "Believe it or not, it's true. Aunt Pearl said she was running around with this boy, and lo and behold, she got preg. Her father paid for an abortion and then threw her out of the house. A couple years later she met Dad. Aunt Pearl doubts that Dad knew about it. Isn't that an interesting tale?"

I felt sick. I still didn't believe it. "Aunt Pearl probably was mad at Mom or something, and made that up."

"Not a bit of it. Pearl is okay. She runs a beauty parlor, and she's a big, hearty, outspoken lady. I'd say no malice there at all. She just thought it was funny Mom married a preacher."

"But to tell *you* — that's really sick."

"Why? 'The truth shall set ye free.' You've heard that a few times, I guess. In a way it did set me free. I don't have to worry any more about offending Mom with my life-style. I just don't intend to listen to her criticisms." She suddenly seemed cheered up again. "And, kiddo, I'm going to live right. Eat, drink, and especially be merry." She got up and began to dress. "Toss me that aqua blouse, will you?"

"It's pretty." I gave it to her. "Where are you going to-night?"

She frowned. "Listen, love, just because you bring me nourishing goodies and listen to my stories doesn't give you the right to check up on me. Does Mom send you out here to spy on me?"

I felt so bad, I couldn't answer her. I started for the door. She caught up with me before I got there and put her arms around me.

"Sissy, I didn't mean it. What a rotten thing to say. Why am I so paranoid?"

"That's okay." I was trying not to cry. I felt battered. First she tells me my mother had an abortion, then she suspects me of spying. What am I supposed to do? Smile?

"Forgive me." She turned my face toward hers. "You're the only real friend I've got, and I do know it, Sis."

So I had to stay a little longer so she wouldn't feel guilty all evening. When I was leaving, she said, "Where did you get that shirt?"

"I don't know. Where do we get anything? It shows up one day in the living room and Mom says, 'See if you can wear this.' "

"Christ!" She said it with so much force, it startled me. "What size are you anyway?"

"Ten, I guess. The question doesn't arise very often."

"That shirt must be a fourteen at least. Oh, God, it makes me sick. Why can't she see what it does to us?"

"It isn't that big a deal." I wanted to get away. What difference did it make about the damned shirt?

"You've got to get out of this town, Sissy. What is the most distant college you could go to?"

I didn't feel like talking about college, but she insisted. "I may be accepted at UCLA, but even with a scholarship I can't afford it."

"Can't you get a federal loan?"

"I don't know."

"Well, find out. Where else could you go?"

"University of Denver."

"Too close. Where else?"

"Some little Bible college in Indiana."

"Oh, shit. Dad's idea, no doubt."

"Sure. But don't worry, I'm not about to go there."

"Sissy, let's work on UCLA. Maybe by that time I can help." She looked at her watch. "But I can't even help myself if I don't get out of here. Look at the time!"

So I left. I felt pretty rotten for a long time. It's not a pleasant thing to be told something like that about your mother. Some kinds of mother, maybe it wouldn't rock you so much. I mean if you knew your mother was kind of a swinger, a real sophisticated type, like Maddie Fleeter's mother, for instance, you might not be so shocked. But *my* mother? It made all her married life seem like a big hunk of hypocrisy. I tried to be understanding and tolerant, I really did, but when I thought about how strict she had always been with us, how disapproving of Charlotte she was right now, it made me sick. For several days I could hardly make myself talk to her at all.

And then one day when I was walking down the street from school to the cafe, Mrs. Fleeter drove by and waved, and all of a sudden I thought, "Mom is scared. If something terrible like that happened to me, something traumatic like getting pregnant and deserted by the guy and kicked out by my family, then I can see being scared silly that my kids might fall into the same trap." I don't know why Mrs. Fleeter made me think of this, except that she is such a with-it lady, so in control of things, you can't imagine her getting into a no-win situation like that, and suddenly Mom seemed vulnerable, and I could see her as a girl my age, trusting some guy and getting clobbered. I felt such a wave of pity, I wanted to run home and do something nice for her. But I had to go to work.

I could tell she was surprised that night at how I knocked myself out to be helpful. I even washed the dishes, which she usually lets me skip when I'm working at the cafe.

While I was washing the dishes, I thought about why she had married Dad, which had always kind of puzzled me, because although she was never mean to him, she didn't show any signs of great love or anything. Perhaps he looked like some kind of sanctuary, after what she had been through.

The next time I saw Charlotte, I tried to say all this to her, but she wouldn't listen. She had a package for me from the May D and F in Denver. There was a brand new pair of blue pants, a couple of blouses, some underwear, and an oyster-white cardigan. I could hardly stand it I was so happy. It wasn't just the beautiful clothes, it was knowing that my sister loved me that much. Robert would have loved me like that, but nobody else did or ever would, I was sure.

She left the next day for Denver and was gone about a week. She stopped in at the cafe to let me know she was back. Something must have gone right. She was wearing all new clothes, and she was aglow.

After she'd gone, Charlie, the cook, said, "Wow, that kid sure turned out to be a smasheroo. She looks like some kind of movie star. She ought to get out of this burg, get a job in television or something."

When I told Charlotte later, she smiled and said, "Who knows." But she didn't give me any clues about what had happened or what she had been doing.

The following Monday when I went to the motel a man I'd never seen before opened the door. "Hi," he said, "if you're selling Girl Scout cookies, I bought at the office." He gave me a big grin. He was kind of good-looking, except that he was about forty and getting a little paunchy like an ex-football player that eats too much and drinks a lot of beer. I thought I must be in the wrong room, so I backed up and looked at the number.

"Are you looking for Charlotte?" he said.

"Yes. I'm her sister." I couldn't imagine who he was. He was in his shirtsleeves and stocking feet, and he was just putting his wristwatch on, fussing with the strap. Without stopping to analyze why I felt that way, I was scared.

"Come in, come in," he said. "I didn't know she had a sister. What's your name?" He was very friendly.

Just then Charlotte came out of the shower wearing her white terrycloth robe. She looked startled when she saw me.

"Sissy! I wasn't expecting you. Uh, Jimmy, this is my sister, Sylvia. Sissy, this is Mr. Korvos."

He held up his hands, laughing. He was certainly a lot more at ease than either Charlotte or I was. "Not Mr. Just Jimmy. Glad to know you, Sissy." He stuck out his hand.

"You're early," Charlotte said.

"I don't work on Mondays."

"Oh, that's right." She seemed nervous and abstracted. "Listen, I'm going out right now. See you tomorrow, all right?"

"Sure," I said. "Of course." I nodded to the man. "I'm glad to've met you, Mr. Korvos."

He laughed. "Jimmy, Jimmy. Glad to have met you too, Sissy. See you around."

I felt terrible. What kind of a family did I come from anyway? It's not that it was so shocking that Charlotte might be having sex with some guy. After all, this isn't the Victorian age. Lots of people are into sex. I knew a bunch of kids at school that went to a motel fairly regularly. It didn't mean a thing to me. And I am not my sister's keeper. But a creep like Korvos? A paunchy forty-year-old jerk that gives you the big ho-ho-call-me-Jimmy and smells of stale cigars? My beautiful sister? I just didn't get it.

I rode my old bike as fast as it would go, and when I cut across the highway, a guy in a car honked his horn and yelled obscenities.

"Up yours, mister." He couldn't hear me, but I was surprised to hear myself because I don't usually talk like that. Not that I care how people talk, but I never have said things like that. Maybe some of my father's ideas did affect me.

I said to myself, "What do you expect, about Charlotte? She's grown up, isn't she? What do you expect — Joan of Arc?"

But the thing was, that's kind of what I did expect. To me she had always been the ideal. I knew she loved to flirt, she had always gone out a lot with guys. Many a time I'd helped her sneak out when Mom had laid a curfew on her. But I guess I hadn't thought about Charlotte and sex. I'd only recently begun to think about it at all. In the last year or so I'd developed some surprising feelings of my own, like turning hot all over when Mr. Jowett smiled at me in the corridor at school — Mr. Jowett, for God's sake! My French teacher, who is even getting a little bald! But I figured that was just hormones or something, and nothing to do with the way I lived my life.

But this was Charlotte. Her life.

My mother was in the kitchen chopping onions. I didn't speak to her. All the sympathy I'd been feeling had gone right down the drain, and I wanted to say, "It's your fault. If you hadn't had your damned abortion, Charlotte wouldn't be sleeping with that fat creep." I knew it didn't make any sense. I went up to my room and put on a Rod Stewart record, loud.

"It gets me toward where I'm going." Charlotte flashed me a smile that said she knew she was talking in circles. "Toward the life I want."

"What life do you want?"

"Sissy! If you keep on cross-examining me, I'll never get out of here. I have to meet Jimmy at seven."

"I'm sorry." I kept quiet for a while and helped her carry her stuff out to the car. "Have you got a place to live?"

"Oh, sure." She wrote down an address. "That's the club. If you need to get in touch. I'm off Sundays and Mondays." She swung her makeup bag onto the car seat and looked at me. "Sissy, I don't mean to evade your questions. I know, boy, do I know! how confusing it all is at your age. But I've got it worked out now. I know what I want and where I'm going." She narrowed her eyes and looked past me, as if she were seeing herself in some glamorous future. "It would take too long to tell you now, but sometime I will. Mainly, though, I just want to be in charge."

"In charge of what?"

"My life. My circumstances. I don't want to be at anybody's beck and call ever again. I am going to call the shots."

"I guess that would be nice." I leaned against the car door. "How does a person get to that point?"

She rubbed her thumb and forefinger together. "Money. Folding green. Bread." She leaned out and kissed my cheek. "I'll be in touch."

I watched her go. I wished it had occurred to her to lend me fifty bucks for my Intention to Enter fee. I wished she had had some advice on where I could raise the folding green for living expenses in Los Angeles. Denver had accepted me, and although I hadn't heard from UCLA yet, I was going to have to make up my mind. The thought of Denver depressed me. Not that it isn't a good college, but it was too close to home. I wanted about a thousand miles, east.

5 ❁ ❁

LATE in April Charlotte moved into Denver. I went to the hotel one afternoon and found her packed and ready to go. She said she intended to let me know. I guess she didn't have to. She always hated goodbyes, and I wasn't her guardian, after all, but I'd have been pretty shook if she had just taken off without a word.

She said that Korvos man had gotten her a job as hoste in a club in Denver, and she would get to do some sing too. She seemed all revved up and happy, so I was glad her, but I felt really empty in my stomach.

I said, "It's temporary, isn't it? I mean there's no future in being a hostess, is there?"

She stopped in the middle of closing her sui looked at me over her shoulder. "Every little you ahead. At least as long as you aren't gall ward or running up and down in one place, a dulge in either of those games."

"But what does it get you *toward?*" I k bug her. She hated to be questioned. But I know, not just for Charlotte but for "ahead" mean? I'm sure my three older were getting ahead when they got ma were, well, just running in place, I had enough money, they had too m didn't amount to much in any ter

About a week later we got the word that two of my sisters, Gertie and Meg, were coming with their husbands and kids for a quick visit en route to the Arches National Monument. They always take their vacations together, usually to some national park. The year before it was Yellowstone. They travel in Meg's and Arthur's van and pitch a tent for the kids.

Mom was pleased, though between them Gert and Meg have seven kids all under nine, and it makes for what could be called pandemonium. My father began making plans to be at a church convention in Pueblo, but Mom squashed that idea.

"You said you didn't want to go to Pueblo."

"Well, I've been thinking . . ."

"I need you here." That ended the discussion.

It isn't that Daddy doesn't like to see Gert and Meg, but so many people in his house unnerved him, and he never has known what to do with children, including his own. Also the husbands drink a lot of beer and cuss a lot.

Meg called up about five times, full of last-minute plan changes and details and confirmations, and she kept asking if we could get Charlotte to come. At first Mom said no, but Meg persisted and finally she got Mom to say she'd see if Charlotte would come out from Denver.

Afterward I said, "Charlotte will want to see them, especially Meg." When Charlotte was my age, I think she looked up to Meg the way I look up to Charlotte. Meg was kind of a rebel as a teenager, sort of a mild hippie. She wore long patchwork skirts and high-heeled clogs, and wore her hair long and stringy. She learned a few chords on the guitar and talked about alternate life-styles and organic food and all that. Arthur was into the same scene. He wore long hair too and a scraggly little beard, and he went barefoot a lot. But all that changed after they got married. He went to work as a meter-reader for the electric company, and had to shave his beard and cut his hair, and they began having babies, and pretty soon they were just like everybody else. Charlotte had missed most of that because for the last four summers she had had jobs away from home.

I was delegated to let Charlotte know they were coming. I dropped her a note to tell her they'd be in town Saturday through Monday, and we all wished she'd come.

On Saturday when I got home from work, they had arrived, and there was a lot of chattering and hugging and laughing going on. Harvey was beside himself with delight. Meg and Gert always seemed self-conscious with him, but their kids liked him, and he adored them. He laughed as hard as they did when they threw him a football and he fell flat on his face trying to catch it.

I didn't feel very close to these people. My sisters had left home when I was young. Everybody looked about the same as last year, except the kids were bigger, and Mervyn had grown a handlebar moustache. He had a new job as assistant manager of a supermarket in this Illinois town where they live, and they looked a little more prosperous. Arthur and Meg had their same old van, faded blue with a dented fender and a painting of a waterfall on the back panel and a bumper sticker that said, "Watch out for the car behind me."

The guys went out and bought buckets and buckets of Colonel Sanders chicken, and four six-packs of beer. Daddy frowned at the beer, and they went through the same teasing routine with him, telling it purified the soul and he ought to try it. Mom had made lemon pies and baked fresh bread and churned up a freezer of ice cream. The kids were squabbling over who got to lick the dasher.

Meg laughed and looked at me. "Remember? We used to fight over the dasher too."

I couldn't remember it with her, but Robert and I used to lay elaborate plans to get hold of it, and we always shared it with each other, and no one else ever got a lick. At least not then. After Robert died, Charlotte had it all to herself.

In the evening they called up our sister, Brenda, who lives near Schenectady, and there was a big hullabaloo while everybody tried to talk to her at once. I got to say hi, but Brenda never comes home and I hardly remember her. Meg and Gert liked her, but they despised her husband, so they never invited her. There's always a lot of talk about how could Brenda have married that Neanderthal creep. He used to be a prizefighter, and he runs a gym. I don't remember ever seeing him.

Mom got on the phone and cried and laughed. Next to Charlotte and Harvey, Brenda was always her favorite. She fielded the questions about Charlotte pretty well. "Working for a consulting firm," she said. "Headquarters in Denver at the moment but she travels a lot." Meg and Gert wanted to call up Charlotte but Mom said we didn't have the number.

Later Meg got me alone and said, "What's with Charl? Is she all right?"

"Sure," I said. "Why not?"

" 'Why not.' " Meg looked irritated. "I just asked. Mom is so vague. And why isn't she in college? Did she flunk out?"

"Of course not. She just didn't like it. It was too poky."

Unexpectedly she laughed. "Now that sounds like Charl. 'Too poky.' She always did like things lively. Do you think she'll come out to see us?"

"Who knows?"

"I don't understand why we can't call her. Don't you have her number or her address?"

"Just where she works, but she doesn't like to be called there." To stall off more questions, I said, "I think she just likes to be left alone, not checked up on all the time by the family."

"Oh. I can understand that all right." She relaxed. "What about you, Sissy? Are you going to make it to college?"

"I guess so."

"Decided where?"

"No, not yet. I'm accepted at Denver."

"Let us know if we can help in any way. We never seem to have any extra cash, but if you wanted to stay with us and go to the junior college, you'd be welcome."

I was touched. I wouldn't live with them for a million dollars, but it was very nice of her to offer.

Long after I went to bed, I heard them talking and laughing and clinking beer cans. The guys set up the tent for the kids near Mom's clothesline, by the hedge. In the middle of the night, when things were quiet at last, I got up and looked out. The moon shone on the blue van like a spotlight, and the tent in the shadows looked unreal, like a cloud caught by the hedge and pinned there.

6 ❀ ☀

ON Sunday it rained, so the backyard barbecue had to take place in the house. It was pure chaos, with Meg and Gertie trying to be helpful in the kitchen, kids underfoot, babies crying, and Mom getting more and more flustered and impatient until finally she ordered everybody out. About half an hour after that clearing of the air, we sat down to eat, us at the dining room table with the leaf in, the kids at the card tables, the babies in high chairs.

When the assorted mothers got their assorted offspring quiet, Daddy began the blessing. It was an especially long one, and in the middle of it the back door opened, and there in the entrance to the diningroom stood Charlotte in a Mata Hari raincoat, with rain dripping off the brim of her high-crowned hat. Daddy never opened his eyes or slowed down, but all the other heads swiveled toward Charlotte. My mother immediately looked down again and shut her eyes and her mouth very tight. Meg made a movement as if to get up, but Arthur touched her arm and she remembered.

Charlotte stood perfectly still with her eyes cast down until Daddy said, "Amen." Then Meg and Gertie jumped up and hugged and kissed Charlotte, and the brothers-in-law shook hands with her, and the kids knocked back their chairs and piled all over her. Harvey beat his spoon handle on the table chanting, "Charla, Charla, Charla."

Charlotte took off her spy coat and her hat and kissed Mom.

"You do make an entrance," Mom said.

Charlotte hugged Daddy and said, "I'm sorry I interrupted the blessing. I didn't realize."

He leaned back and looked at her through his bifocals. "The Lord was not distracted," he said.

"No, I suppose not."

"Charlie, sit down," Meg said; "tell us everything. It's so wonderful to see you. You look like a movie star. Jenny, give Aunt Charlotte your chair."

Five-year-old Jenny began to wail a protest, and Arthur gave her a slap that brought on screams.

"To your room!" Meg was red in the face. "This minute."

"Haven't got a room," Jenny sobbed.

Charlotte picked her up and rocked her while she talked to Meg and Gert, and in a minute Jenny was silent, thumb in mouth, gazing in fascination at her new aunt.

Charlotte said she had eaten, and all she wanted was some of Mom's good coffee. I got her a cup, and she gave me a quick smile.

The rest of the evening went on at a high decibel of sound. Ordinary speech is about 190 decibels. Add a zero and it would be somewhere close to the level that evening. I didn't even try to follow any of the conversations. Gertie's oldest boy, who is named Robert, went down cellar with me, and we tossed a softball back and forth until it hit a jar of Mom's tomato preserve. It was last year's preserve, and it wouldn't have been all that good any more. Robert and I cleaned it up and made a pact not tell. It felt strange to be playing ball and having secrets with someone named Robert.

Around ten o'clock, when all the kids had finally been stashed away in their tent, I walked with Charlotte out to the alley where she had left her car.

"Hey, you've got a new car."

"It's Jimmy's." She looked tired, and she stopped a minute and leaned one hand against Meg's van. She lifted her face to the rain, and with a sudden scrubbing motion she wiped her mouth. "Mervyn kissed me."

"He's a big kisser."

She shuddered and stepped back to look at the faded painting on the van. "Dear God," she said, in a low, kind of despairing voice, "Niagara Falls."

"They're all right, though," I said. "Meg especially."

Charlotte had a faraway look. "I used to think Meg was going to bust loose and be somebody. A real rebel."

"Well, I suppose she's somebody to herself and to her family and all."

She looked angry all of a sudden. "You call that being somebody? *That?*" She jerked her head toward the house. Raindrops rolled off her hatbrim and down her face. "That's pure shit."

She slammed the door of Jimmy's car, and I didn't know whether to say goodnight or not, but then she grabbed my hand and held it against her cheek and said, "Don't let it happen to you, Sissy. You're smart. Get out of here and be somebody."

She was gone before I could say "What kind of somebody?"

7 ❋ ❋

IT was almost the first of May and graduation was coming at me like some kind of express train. On the day that my acceptance at UCLA came, I was in a real dither. I wanted so much to go, but I just could not figure it, even with a scholarship and a loan. Living expenses were horrendous.

Maddie Fleeter got her acceptance too, and money was no problem with her, but she still hadn't made up her mind. Her father wanted her to go there. He had been a football star, and he was very gung-ho about the university. And they about him, I guess. That was what turned Maddie off. She was sick of hearing about UCLA. So we were on our way into Denver to look over the campus. I positively had to make my decision right away. I was wishing I had a problem as simple as hers.

Maddie was my best friend in school. I had out-of-school friends, like Jan Baker, whose house I stayed at now and then, and who went to the movies with me sometimes, that sort of thing. But Maddie and I were strictly school-hours friends. I had been to her house only once, when she gave a party for the whole class, sophomore year. She had never been to my house. For one thing, she lived out in the country, on a farm that her mother had inherited, Charlotte called it a reconstituted farm. The Fleeters did the big house over, put in a rec room and a sauna, a swimming pool, tennis court, a riding ring, all that. Both of them were lawyers. Mr. Fleeter was a criminal lawyer and he zipped all around the country in his own Lear jet. Mrs. Fleeter had an office in Denver, and drove in every day in her nifty Audi Fox. My mother liked to say, with a sniff of disapproval, "They are not our kind of people." Charlotte thought she said that because Mrs. Fleeter got to do all the things Mom would have liked to do — Bermuda every year, Las Vegas, Chivas Regal after dinner, clothes from Saks Fifth Avenue, et cetera. Mom would have denied it to her last breath, but now that I knew more about her, I thought Charlotte might be right.

Anyway Maddie and I looked over the Denver campus. It was nice enough and they were supposed to have a good language department, but somehow it seemed too much like home. Charlotte was right, I needed to break loose.

Maddie and I went downtown in her VW and had lunch at Bauer's. I didn't let her know what a rare treat this was for me. I could count my trips to Denver on one and a half hands. She bought the lunch.

Maddie is a tall, kind of gawky kid, with hair so blonde and fine it looks like white silk. She has acne scars, and a big nose, and she's allergic to almost everything. She sees herself as a total disaster, but she is funny about it. I really like her. We laugh a lot.

She asked me, if she went to UCLA, would I go too. I tried to make her understand it was a question of money, but she has so much money, it's hard for her to take that seriously. She seemed to think I was just being thrifty, and she kept saying, "But Sissy, it's worth it." Well, it may be worth the money if you have the money, but if you don't have it, it's moot.

We talked about our school annual, which had just come out. My picture looked spaced-out. Alice Dunham had written the captions, and for mine she wrote, "She searches the imponderable stars. 'Of the wide world I stand alone and think, Till love and fame to nothingness do sink.' "

Maddie repeated it, as we were eating our deviled crabs, and she said, "I heard Miss Winship say to Alice, 'For the love of heaven, Alice, if you're going to quote Keats, quote Keats. Don't try to improve on him with gems of your own.' "

We laughed like mad, because we don't like Alice.

My prophecy said, "Sissy will go far in her quiet way. Holding life's clay in her capable hands, she will mold it to her heart's desire." What garbage!

"But listen to mine," Maddie said. " 'Maddie is headed for the Riviera, Paris, Hong Kong, the Land of Oz.' Jesus! What is that supposed to mean?"

"It means you're loaded." It was a tactless thing to say. She turned red, as if I had insulted her. "I don't know about that Oz bit." I was trying to talk my way out of it. "That must mean you're searching for something."

"I'm searching for a husband that looks like Erik Estrada. Want to make any bets?" She meant she'd never get one. She had convinced herself that men didn't like her, though she always had them hanging around. She thought it was the swimming pool and the tennis court they came for.

"Come on, Mad," I said. "If you want him, you'll get him. You're a very determined kid."

"Sure," she said, and got kind of morose, the way she does sometimes. We had ice cream in a meringue with hot fudge sauce, and she cheered up a little.

The next day I got a check from Charlotte with a note saying I was to buy myself a dress for the commencement dance. It was a wonderful surprise, but a bit of a problem. When you have bought clothes as seldom as I had, shopping can be pretty unnerving. I must have tried on every formal in the Merc and in the Young Miss Boutique, plus several dozen in Fort Collins. Finally I made up my mind and then worried about shoes, lipstick, eyeshadow (to wear or not to wear), what to do with my hair, which is short and brown and totally without character. I had fantasies of dying it red or doing a white streak up the middle of my head. I kept wondering if the money Charlotte sent had come from What's-his-name.

I don't know if it was the effect of the new clothes or not, but I took fifty of my last seventy bucks out of my bureau drawer and got a postal money order and sent it off to UCLA. It was insane; I couldn't possibly go there. But I did it. I also turned down Denver. What I would really do, I felt fairly sure, was go to a junior college in Los Angeles. Even for out-of-state kids, it was very inexpensive, and you didn't have to stand in line months in advance. Once I had said no to Denver, I felt better.

On the night of the dance, in spite of or maybe because of my new dress, I felt very self-conscious. In social situations I always feel that other people know things I don't know. I almost chickened out altogether, but then there came Dana Ross clutching one long-stemmed yellow rose and looking almost as nervous as I was. My hands were clammy, and I nearly tore my dress trying to pin the rose on. By the time it was attached, both Dana and I were wrecks.

Dana has been my friend since the first grade, and I think he asked me to the dance because he was just as scared as I was. He's good-looking, but very shy. He's afraid of girls. I'm afraid of boys. We feel safe with each other.

It was a nice dance, I guess, although whenever Dana danced with other girls, I was so scared I wouldn't get asked that I fled to the girls' room. Girls kept pouncing on him, and he'd give me this helpless look while he was being dragged off. He had a perfect right to dance with other girls, naturally.

At intermission I spilled orange sherbet on the front of my dress.

But the real bummer was graduation day. All day I'd been hoping to hear from Charlotte. When she sent me the check for the dress, I wrote her right back and asked her to come, but I hadn't heard another word. The note with the check just said, "Sissy darlin', I'm busy as a birddog so excuse hasty note. Buy yourself a glamorous dress and knock 'em dead. All my love, Charlotte."

"There's no use you looking for Charlotte to come," my mother said, although I hadn't mentioned it. "She won't come clear out here for a high school graduation, not even yours."

"I know that." But just the same I looked out the window every time a car drove by. And Harvey nearly sent me crazy because he kept looking too and saying, "Charla'll come," over and over.

It was a hot day, and our caps and gowns were like a sauna. For some never-explained reason we had to stand forever in the sun before we got the signal to march into the auditorium. I tripped over my gown on the steps and heard a rip, but there was no chance to check it.

Mom had Harvey in his wheelchair near the back, and when he saw me, he began clapping his hands in time to Mrs. Aune's organ music. Somebody giggled, and I felt like hitting them, only I didn't know who it was, so I couldn't even give them a dirty look. Mom grabbed Harvey's hands, and I gave him the biggest smile I could manage when I marched by.

Daddy gave the invocation, and as usual went on too long but he said some interesting things, I thought. I could see kids stealing despairing glances at each other. I was supposed to have my eyes closed, setting a good example like the minister's kids should, but I didn't miss anything.

Then there was a speech by the dean of a teachers' college in Kansas, all about finding our way in this troubled world, keeping our eyes on the goal, ad astra per aspera, and all that jazz. And that *really* went on forever. I was having trouble not yawning. Maddie caught my eye and yawned behind her hand and just barely stifled a giggle when the yawn caught me too. It's very contagious, yawning. I tried not to look at Maddie because I was afraid I'd bust out laughing.

Then the prizes were given out, and I had to step up and collect the English prize, the *Collected Poems* of Robert Frost. I was sure the rip in my gown must be showing, but there was nothing I could do except suffer. We all filed by to get our diploma in one hand and the other hand shaken by the principal, and then at last we were out in the fresh air, and people were grinning all over their faces and saying "Congratulations, congratulations, congratulations." I got special gush from certain types that always think it's absolutely incredible when the minister's kids do anything right.

Still Charlotte hadn't come, and I'd have given up the English prize and a lot else to look up and see my sister standing there with that smile that lights up the world.

The same day, I got word that I could have a job at the cafe six hours a day. So it would be a summer at home.

Right after I'd gone to bed that night, the phone rang. I didn't figure it would be for me, but then Mom was calling me. "Sissy. Phone."

It was a person-to-person call, the first one I ever got in my life, probably the last.

It was Charlotte, sounding bubbly and happy, telling me she was proud of me and she wished she could have been there and how did it go. Then she said, "Guess where I am."

"Hollywood?"

"No."

"Denver?"

"No." She giggled.

"So tell me."

She made one of her dramatic pauses and said, "Las Vegas."

"You're kidding!"

"No, honestly. I'm phoning from the bar. I'm sipping a long tall drink with pineapple and cherries and God knows what in it, and I never felt more debauched or happier in my life."

I had to laugh. "You are the most. How did it happen?"

"You remember Jimmy?"

"Sure."

"Well, he's bought an interest in a small club here, and I'm going to keep the books and also I get to sing, late at night, in the piano bar."

I couldn't believe it. How many people have sisters that sing in a piano bar in Las Vegas? I tried to tell her how impressed I was.

"Listen, I've got to hang up now but I'll be in touch. Tell Mom I'll call her, maybe next week."

"Don't you want to speak to her?"

Her voice changed a little. "Not now, Sis. I've got to run. Stay happy." And she was gone.

Mom looked up when I went into the living room. "Charlotte?"

"Yes. She said she'd call you next week. She sent you her love." I knew Mom would be hurt, and I didn't blame her.

"Since when does she call person-to-person? That costs. Was she afraid she might have to talk to me?"

"Oh, Mom, don't be silly. It's my graduation, she wanted to congratulate me. And if I hadn't been here, she'd have had to call again."

"Is she still in Denver?"

"No, she left."

"Well, where is she?"

"Las Vegas." I saw her look of shock so I kept talking. "She says it's really cool. Swimming pools and everything."

My mother set her face like a stone. "Corruption," she said.

"Oh, come on, that's not fair." I don't usually argue with her, but that made me mad. "How can you label a city like that?"

"The Bible labeled Sodom and Gomorrah. I can label Las Vegas."

"But you aren't exactly in the same category with the Bible, are you, Mom?" I was sorry as soon as I said it. "Hey, I didn't mean that. Only Charlotte sounded so happy. I hate to hear you condemn her when there's nothing to condemn. . . ."

She interrupted me. "You shouldn't argue about things you know nothing about. Go to your room." She raised her voice slightly. "Now."

I went to my room. Sissy, the family baby, the stupid one that anybody can push around. Go to your room and shut your ignorant stupid mouth. High school graduate, honor roll student, English prizewinner, almost eighteen years old, and a big nothing. I picked up the first thing that was handy and threw it hard across my room. Glass shattered. And then I saw what I'd done. I had smashed the Coke bottle that Charlotte painted flowers on when she was in the eighth grade. The pussy willows I'd put in it when she came home were scattered on the floor, and there was a damp spot on the rug where the last of the water had spilled.

8 ❋ ❋

WHAT I remember most about that summer is blistering heat and drought, the day Harvey broke my grandmother's vase, and the thunderstorm that turned Fort Lewis into a sodden mess.

Every day we sweltered. At noon I went to the café and worked till nine at night. All summer I felt as if I were swimming in hot water and not getting anywhere.

The day Harvey broke the vase, I walked to the cafe with Dana. He had a job as lifeguard at the town pool, and I envied him. He pointed out that he never got to swim except for a quick plunge after the pool closed. Still he could wear swim trunks and a shade hat and at least look at the water. I was feeling sorry for myself.

"You're the color of my mother's mahogany sewing table," I said, "and look at me, a beautiful shade of curdled milk."

Charlotte had just written me. She had moved from the high life in Vegas to the high life in Hollywood. Her letter was very short as usual, and she didn't tell me much, but she sounded happy, almost too happy, too keyed up. She mentioned that she was singing in a little club in West Hollywood now and then. She didn't say anything about Jimmy Korvos.

Dana asked me where Charlotte was, and when I told him,

he said, "Oh." I had the feeling he didn't approve of my going to college in the same city where Charlotte was, and that irritated me. It was none of his business. I knew I would feel better if I was near to her so I could make sure she was all right. Which was pretty funny, I guess, since she had always been so much more competent and sure of herself than I ever was.

When I went into the diner, I said over to myself Pindar's Eighth Ode, that Mr. Connolly had translated for us the last week of school, his moustache twitching like mad.

> *Man's life is a day. What is he, what is he not?*
> *Man is the dream of a shadow. But when the god-given*
> > *brightness comes,*
> *A bright light is among men, and an age that is gentle*
> > *comes to birth.*

I kept going over it in my mind because it sounded so hopeful. I was not at all sure I believed in that god-given brightness, but maybe Pindar knew something I didn't know.

There were stacks of hamburgers to be fried partway through so they'd be cooked fast when somebody ordered, and I soon forgot Pindar, but the smell of frying grease still reminds me of that summer.

When I got home that night, everybody was in a state. Harvey was sitting on the floor sobbing and rocking back and forth. Mom was trying to glue together her mother's hand-painted bud vase, and tears were streaming down her face. Dad had fled to the church office. I couldn't get either of them to tell me what had happened, but Harvey's softball that Charlotte gave him was on the floor, and I could picture the scene. He's not supposed to play with it in the house, and every time he does, Mom gets mad at Charlotte for having given it to him.

I was dog-tired, and since I couldn't do either of them

48

any good, I went upstairs and flopped on my bed. I was glad it was near the end of summer. Very, very glad. The junior college I had written to was Valley College, in the San Fernando Valley. It seemed to have a very good selection of courses, and maybe the Valley wouldn't be quite so big-city and scary as Los Angeles proper. Not that I knew anything about it, never having been there. I planned to go out a couple of weeks before registration, so I could look for a place to live. A rooming house or whatever. It was pretty terrifying to think about, not knowing my way around or knowing anyone to ask except Charlotte, and I was not about to get her to help. I wanted to be all settled before I even let her know I was coming. I was not going to be a burden to her.

I had thought an awful lot about her relationship with Korvos, and I had decided she saw it as a means to an end. Personally I don't think any end is justified by a lousy means; sooner or later you pay for the means. The most significant piece of advice (one of the few) my father ever gave me was when he said, "There's no such thing as a free lunch." I believe it. Maybe Charlotte would prove me wrong, but I worried about her.

I fell asleep with my clothes on, and was waked up an hour or two later by a great smash of thunder. My curtains were blowing all over the place and the rain was soaking the floor. I was so relieved by the coolness, I got up and knelt by the window and let the rain beat on my face.

That's where my mother found me when she came in to make sure I'd waked up and closed the windows. I guess she was still unhappy about the vase, because she was unusually mad at me about letting it rain in. She banged down the windows and threw a towel at me to mop up the water and said I was a slob for going to sleep in my clothes and how much longer was I going to hang around the house making work for her.

By the time she left, I wasn't feeling so great. I mopped up the damned rain and got undressed and brushed my teeth. With the windows closed, it was almost as hot as it had been before. Finally I did something that was more like Charlotte than like me. I put on my raincoat over my pajamas, sneaked down the back stairs, and sat on the back porch. Every time the lightning flashed, I could hear Harvey howl. He was terrified of thunder and lightning. Poor Harvey. He could never get away. But I could.

9 ❀ ❀

By morning the thunderstorm had turned into a heavy rain and wind storm, and the town seemed to have become one big mud pie. I wore my rubber boots (two sizes too big, courtesy of Mrs. Farley's oldest daughter's teenager), and by the time I got to the cafe, I was muddy to my knees, and my raincoat (courtesy of Jennie Farrell) was wet through.

But the change in the weather was a relief. We kidded Dana about being a lifeguard in pouring rain.

Maddie came in during my ten-minute break. She had been in Hawaii with her family. She had a super tan. They had been on Maui and she said it was great, but she seemed depressed. She still was resisting UCLA, though she was officially in. Now she wanted to go to the University of Hawaii, but her family wouldn't let her.

"I know I'll hate Los Angeles."

"We can get together for a yak session now and then. I'll be in the San Fernando Valley."

"I'm still battling with my family. If I have to go to UCLA, I want my own apartment, and Mom is bound and determined not to let me have it. She says I have to live in the dorm."

"Is that so bad?"

"I don't want to go from one prison to another. I want

51

my own place. I'm eighteen, for God's sake. I know what I'm doing. She just doesn't trust me. Well, keep in touch, Sissy. I'm glad you're going to Los Angeles anyway." She went off with that long-legged graceful lope of hers. She looks like a great tennis player type, and she is. I found it hard to understand why she cared so much about having her own apartment. My mother had hardly mentioned to me where I was going to live. It would have been nice if she had worried a little.

The next night when I got through work, I saw Maddie's mother parked in her Audi Fox. It had stopped raining, but it takes a while for our streets to drain. It was still pretty sloppy walking. Across the street Olsen's drugstore had had a plate glass window blown in by the wind, and his sign was hanging crooked. It looked like Main Street as seen in a bad dream. I waved to Mrs. Fleeter and started up the street, but she leaned out the window and said, "Sissy, can I speak to you a minute?"

I was stunned. She is always pleasant, but I had never said more than hello to her in my life. I went back to the car, and she said, "Get in. I'll drive you home."

She is a tall, dark lady, with beautiful clothes. I wished she gave *her* castoff clothes to the minister's kids, but she is too tall for me anyway. She wears more makeup than most women in Fort Lewis, but on her it looks good. She was smoking a cigarette in a long ivory holder. I wondered if she had considered lung cancer.

"I was waiting for you," she said. "I want to talk to you."

What had I done wrong now?

She glanced at me and said, "Don't be alarmed." I guess lawyers learn to read your face. She started up her gorgeous car and drove slowly up the street. The leather upholstery felt cool and smelled like tangerines. A tape deck was playing very low; it sounded like Beethoven, and I thought of Harvey.

"Maddie tells me you've decided on Valley College."

"Yes, I have."

"With your grades, Sissy, you ought to be at UCLA or USC or some university like that."

"I hope I'll be able to transfer junior year. If I get good enough grades."

She talked with her cigarette holder clamped between her teeth, and a pale blue cloud of smoke wreathing her face. She squinted her eyes against the smoke. "Maddie is going to UCLA, and of course her dad is all for it."

"I'm sure she'll like it."

"Well, I'm the fly in the ointment, I'm afraid. Maddie wants her own apartment, insists on it. I don't go for that idea at all. I think she's too young and much too unused to life in a city like Los Angeles. She's a small-town girl, after all."

I had never thought of Maddie as a small-town girl. "She's traveled a lot."

"Yes, but with us. She's never had any responsibility." She looked sideways at me. "Did you apply for grants, scholarships, that sort of thing, at UCLA?"

"Yes. They would give me a scholarship and I could get a grant, but none of that was enough to cover all my tuition and room and board." I couldn't imagine why she was asking me this stuff.

When we got to my house she stopped and swiveled around toward me. I could smell her perfume; it smelled expensive. "You wonder what I'm driving at. I'll tell you. The only way I would consider letting Maddie have her own digs would be to have her share a place with someone we knew and trusted. When she mentioned your interest in UCLA, Roy and I looked at each other and said, 'Ideal.'"

I felt as if there were some point I was missing. "But I really can't consider UCLA this year. I've told them. I've worn out about ten pencils adding up expenses and all, and I can't do it." Hadn't I just said that?

"But if it could be arranged, Sissy. My husband has all

kinds of pull there. They still think of him making those forty-yard runs, and of course he gives them outrageously big gifts. He could arrange to get you a better scholarship deal or a grant or whatever you need, and if you lived with Maddie, you wouldn't have any rent to pay. Would you consider it?"

"No rent to pay?"

Her patience began to slip. "That's what I'm talking about, Sissy. We would like you to share an apartment with Maddie. We feel you would be a good influence."

The minister's daughter, I thought.

"It wouldn't cost you a dime for rent."

I really couldn't quite take it in. Did people do things like this?

"Well?"

"Gosh," I said, "I don't think my mother would let me."

"I'll come in and talk to her." She got out of the car before I could answer and strode up the walk that needed weeding, to the front door that needed painting, and rang the bell that doesn't ring.

I caught up with her and opened the door. "Mother," I called out, to give Mom warning, "there's someone to see you."

My mother was in the living room still struggling with the pieces of the broken vase. She had glued it together the night before, but apparently it fell apart again. She looked hot and exasperated. Harvey sat on the sofa, on the edge, staring at her with worried eyes.

"Who is it?" my mother said. She didn't sound welcoming.

"It's Mrs. Fleeter." I was worried about what her reaction would be, but she surprised me. She looked flustered. I have very seldom seen my mother flustered in that way. She's usually pretty cool with people, after nearly a lifetime of dealing with all the types that wander into a minister's house. But she pushed her hair back and wiped her hands on her apron and almost but not quite stammered, "Mrs. Fleeter. Come in."

Mrs. Fleeter was already in. I saw Harvey wrinkle his nose and then smile with pleasure as the scent of her perfume reached him.

"Afternoon, Mrs. Duncan. Hello, Harvey." She gave him a brilliant smile. "Oh, you've broken your lovely hand-painted vase."

She couldn't have said anything more likely to win Mom over. "It was my mother's," she said. "I can't seem to glue it so it stays."

"Harvey broke," Harvey said, rocking a little.

"It was an accident," Mother said.

"Of course it was." Mrs. Fleeter picked up the bottle of glue. "Here's your trouble, Mrs. Duncan. Wrong kind of glue."

"Wrong kind? It says it glues everything."

"But it doesn't. I had a lovely Italian glass pitcher, when we were living in San Francisco — Venetian glass, you know — and it broke. I took it to a wonderful little Japanese man who said to me, 'Grue eat grass.' "

Mom looked blank.

Mrs. Fleeter laughed. "He meant 'Glue eats glass,' and he was absolutely right. But now there's a very good glue that doesn't eat glass. Here, let me write down the name of it for you." She rummaged around in her purse and brought out a memo pad and a silver fountain pen.

Mother was looking completely bewildered. Here was the richest woman in the county in our living room writing down the name of some kind of glue that didn't eat glass, sounding like a TV commercial. I felt like giggling, but I managed to stay serious. I knew as soon as Mom heard what Mrs. Fleeter was here for, that would be the end of this little scene. She'd say no, and Mrs. Fleeter would go away, case lost. I could imagine my mother afterward saying "Let my daughter live on Fleeter charity? No way."

"I hope you'll forgive me for just barging in like this," Mrs. Fleeter was saying, using all her charm. "I wanted to talk to you about Sissy's college."

"Sissy's college?" Mom looked at me suspiciously, to see if I had been holding out on her.

"Yes. I want someone dependable to share an apartment with Maddie at UCLA."

"But she isn't going to UCLA. It's too expensive."

Harvey had gotten up and sidled over to Mrs. Fleeter. He said, "You smell pretty."

She smiled. "Thank you, dear."

My mother turned slightly red and said, "Sissy, take Harvey into the kitchen, please, and fix him a sandwich."

I didn't want to leave; the conversation concerned me, after all. But when my mother said go, I went. I dragged Harvey with me. He didn't want to leave either, but the prospect of a peanut butter and banana sandwich persuaded him. He sat silently clapping his hands together, while I fixed the sandwich. Then he took a huge bite and got peanut butter and mashed banana all over his wide, smiling face. I felt suddenly homesick for him, before I'd even left home. I made him some chocolate milk to show him how much I loved him.

I'd have liked to hear what was going on in the living room, but our old parsonage is too well built for eavesdropping. I kept expecting to hear the slam of the door and the roar of the Audi, but they didn't come. Finally I heard their voices in the hall, and now I could hear what they were saying. I couldn't believe how friendly my mother sounded.

"...a great opportunity for our daughter," my mother was saying. It took a second to realize she meant me. I had never heard her refer to anyone but Charlotte as "our daughter."

56

And Mrs. Fleeter said, "I'll be in touch after Roy talks to the admissions office. He'll fix everything. She'll have more papers to make out, I'm sure, but we can help her with them. It's mostly routine."

Goodbyes and thank-you-very-much, and then the gentle closing of the door, and the roar of the Audi.

My mother was smiling, as if she had triumphed somehow. She didn't look at me right away, but she said to Harvey, "Well, your little sister pulled it off. I didn't think she had it in her."

"Sissy made me a good sandwich," Harvey said, jamming the last of it into his mouth. "Good Sissy. I love Sissy."

"What did I pull off?" I said to my mother.

"UCLA. A student loan, without me having to lift a finger. A rent-free apartment."

"I thought you didn't approve of the Fleeters."

"Approve? Of course I approve. I never said I didn't approve. Wait till your father hears this. He won't believe it. He didn't think you were going to college at all."

I hadn't talked to them much about it, because they hadn't seemed interested. Now I understood why she was so pleased. She was going to get rid of me. She hadn't believed I was really going away, and she had been afraid she was going to be stuck with me. Now everything was solved and she had not had to do a thing.

"Nobody has asked me whether I want to do this."

She looked amazed. "Want to do it? Sissy, even you are not so unreasonable as not to want a solid gold college career dropped in your lap."

"No, I guess not," I said. "Even me." I went upstairs and left her to her wild enthusiasm.

10 ❀ ❀

As my mother pointed out, there was nothing at all that I had to do except sign my name a few times to UCLA documents. The Fleeters moved like computers, zip, zip, zip, push a button, sign a paper, make a phone call, zip, zip, zip. Sissy was in.

Maddie and her mother went to Los Angeles to find an apartment in Westwood, which is the Los Angeles village where UCLA is. "Los Angeles is a collection of small towns." I think eleven different people told me that. Maddie reported that our apartment was fantastic. Mrs. Fleeter told my mother it was close to campus, large, with two bedrooms, kitchen, et cetera, and was suitable. The idea of a separate bedroom was a relief. I had never had a room of my own till Charlote moved away, but once I got used to it, I couldn't bear to think of not having one anymore.

I was excited about UCLA, but I wasn't absolutely comfortable in my mind. Although Mrs. Fleeter made it sound as if I were doing them a big favor to live with Maddie, actually in terms of dollars and cents *she* was doing *me* a big favor. It was the same old charity-for-the-minister's-kid routine that I had been stuck with all my life. I tried to talk to Dana about it one day, since he was the only person who could possibly understand what I meant, but he said I was silly.

59

"The Fleeters have so much money, they won't even miss it. Anyway they have to pay Maddie's rent somewhere."

"But I'm getting a free ride."

"Why not? I wish somebody would pay my room at Boulder. My father is complaining already."

Later Mr. Connolly stopped me on the street. "Sissy, I'm so pleased that you're going to UCLA."

I thanked him.

"I hope you'll major in classical languages. You have a real flair. I've never had a better Latin student."

I was so overwhelmed, I stopped to talk to him for a few minutes, something I would normally never have done. "I've been worrying about what to major in. I love Latin, but the classics don't have much future these days, do they?" I realized it was not a tactful thing to say. It was his field after all.

But he didn't seem to mind. "Forget about 'future.' There'll always be a 'future' for the classics, I should hope. God help us if there isn't. But with so many people feeling there isn't, all too few are training for it. I think you'd find the field limited but wide open, if you see what I mean." He was looking very earnest, his moustache twitching and his forehead wrinkled up in an anxious frown. I felt as if I ought to reassure him.

"My mother wants me to take business ed," I said.

He clapped his hand to his head. "Oh, God. Sissy, I shouldn't say this, but I'm going to. I've said it to other bright kids. Don't, repeat don't, let your parents tell you what to major in or how to live your life. They mean well, but they have many mixed motives they don't even understand themselves. Just smile sweetly and don't argue, but do it your way. Will you promise me that?"

I was amused and touched that he cared what I did. "Sure, I'll promise that."

He held out his hand. "Shake."

60

We shook, and he sped off, looking worried as he always did. I wondered if his mother tried to tell him what to do with his life, and whether she succeeded.

I wanted to go to California on the bus. I had enough money, and I wanted to see the country. But before I even heard about it, it was all decided that I would go with Maddie and her father in the Lear jet. I objected, and my mother looked as if I'd gone right round the bend.

"Most girls would be beside themselves with joy to be flying to the coast in a private plane. I don't know, Sissy, whether you're congenitally ungrateful, or whether you just like to sound contrary."

"I just like to make my own decisions now and then."

She rocked hard in her chair (she must be the last modern mother with her own rocking chair) and bit off the darning thread that she was patching Harvey's socks with. "I hope you aren't going to get ideas like your sister's."

That made me mad. "Which sister?" I said, as if I didn't know.

"Your sister Charlotte, of course," she snapped. "Too big for her britches, that girl is."

"Why? Because she didn't carry out your plans for her?"

She looked surprised. I don't usually talk back to her.

"I just hope," she said, "you'll remember who you are. It won't get you anywhere to get big ideas about yourself. Just because the Fleeters have taken you up, don't think the world is an easy place."

"I've never had any reason to think so."

"The modern world is full of temptations for a young girl."

"Wasn't it always?"

She gave me a fierce stare. I could almost see her wondering if Charlotte had told me what Aunt Pearl had said. "No, it was not. All this drinking and dope and permissiveness . . ."

I wanted to throw her words back at her. How could she sit there and be so righteous?

"The Age of Innocence," she said. "There was a book by that name."

"I know, Mom."

"People knew each other. If a person was in trouble, someone would help. Nowadays nobody cares. A girl could get raped, get into terrible trouble, and nobody would care."

So that was the story. She'd been raped? That wasn't what Aunt Pearl told Charlotte. I didn't say anything.

"I want you to stay away from Charlotte out there in California."

"Stay away from Charlotte?"

"That's what I said. Goodness only knows what kind of life she's living." She began to cry silently. "I want you to promise me."

"I can't promise that. I love Charlotte."

"Love has nothing to do with it."

"Of course I'll see her."

She stood up, letting the darning fall to the floor. "I should have known it was no use asking you one small favor." She left the room in tears.

11 ❀ ❀

As they say, don't leave home without it. Your own Lear jet, that is. We were in LAX almost before I had found enough nerve to look out the window. I'd flown only once before, to Omaha, when my Grandmother Duncan died, and that was altogether different. Being in a small plane is more like being up there with nothing but your own arms flapping in the air to keep you up.

At least that was how *I* felt. Mr. Fleeter and Maddie seemed to take it all for granted. Mr. Fleeter flew the thing himself, and since he does it all the time, I guess it's no more of a big deal to him than driving a car.

Maddie was all keyed up about UCLA, but I hadn't gotten to that yet. I can only take one piece of excitement at a time. After we got off the plane, there was that enormous airport to react to, and then the city itself. From all you hear and read about Los Angeles, I expected solid smog. But it happened to be a beautiful day, about seventy degrees with a breeze, and no smog at all that I could see. And the city looked beautiful. Mr. Fleeter rented a car from Hertz, who seemed to know him (everywhere we went, people knew him), and before we went to Westwood, he gave us a tour through Hollywood, across on La Cienega to Wilshire and through Beverly Hills and Bel Air, pointing out movie and TV stars' houses, and finally to Westwood.

Now I was ready for UCLA. Only I had to take that in short steps too, there was so much to absorb. First we went to the campus, and got the Fleeter grand tour: where he had lived when he was an undergraduate, where he had taken favorite courses, where he made those forty-yard runs. Then he took us to the administration building, got a big hello from various people, and introduced his daughter and his daughter's friend. We picked up a thousand cards and papers, and signed a thousand cards and papers, and were told when and where to go for registration. It was all so overwhelming, I began to feel disembodied, as if I could see and hear everyone, but they couldn't hear or see me. I was the shadow hovering behind Maddie, too scared to open my mouth.

At last we came to our apartment. Mr. Fleeter was in a hurry because he had to see a client, but he was coming back later to take us to dinner. Maddie and I put our suitcases down — she had seven, I had two — and looked around. Maddie had seen it before, but she was just as excited as if she had not. She stretched her arms over her head and stood on her toes and said, "Ours! *No* parents, *no* adults. Sissy, we've made it."

It surprised me that a person who lived on an estate with her own horses and swimming pool and car should feel a need to escape, but I guess I had a lot to learn about other people. I certainly had a tremendous feeling of escape myself. I began to understand how Charlotte had felt, and why she stayed away.

The apartment was big and attractive. It must have cost the Fleeters a mint. The living room had a fireplace that worked, and big squashy chairs and sofa. The kitchen was small but everything looked almost new, and there was a big breakfast nook. We each had a bedroom with tiny vine-covered balcony, and a bath between the rooms. I opened my casement windows, feeling like Juliet or Keats, and looked out at trees and people's patios. We were on a slight hill on the other side of the road from the campus. It was really a big house that had been made into three apartments for students.

We were too excited to finish any one thing, so we alternated unpacking, wandering around, making coffee, talking. Maddie went outside and came back to report she had already met two of the other tenants, and that there was a patio with a big Weber barbecue that we could all use. I went out and looked at it. It was yellow. You could cook a whole roast on the spit. At our house we had a couple of those round wire and tin deals that you set on the ground and cook in. They cost three-fifty apiece at the Coast-to-Coast. How the other half lives.

When Mr. Fleeter came back in the evening, he brought Maddie a ten-speed Schwinn. I could see him wondering if he should have gotten one for me too. Who needs it? The only bike I had ever had in my life was an old wreck that my sisters had when they were kids, and it was okay. It got me where I wanted to go.

He took us to Chasen's for dinner, and pointed out vaguely familiar-looking people that I thought I'd seen in movies or on the TV. A couple of them came over to talk to him, and he introduced us. I really felt dazed. The food was wonderful but I was too revved up to eat much. But the nicest thing about Mr. Fleeter was the way he talked to us, as if we were grown up. He told us about some of his cases, and he was fascinating. I wished Charlotte could hear him.

About three days before we left, a card had come for me from Charlotte, one of her usual shorthand-type messages: "What college? Let me know. All is fabulous here. Love, C." And she added a Beverly Hills post office box number. When my mother saw it, she just clamped her mouth and said nothing. I wrote the box number in my address book and left the card for her. Charlotte was always so "Come on and stay away." If she really wanted to see me, why a post office box?

The first week was hectic. Figuring out schedules, talking to advisors, registering, going to freshmen meetings, getting settled in the apartment. I had never gone through anything like it. It was scary and fascinating. So many people. That was the part that interested me most: all the different people from all over the world.

I was taking American lit, French, Latin, and sociology, and I could hardly wait to get started. But somewhere in the middle of all the busyness, I did send Charlotte a short letter. I had checked the phone books and couldn't find her listed, so I had to write. Maybe she'd never answer. All right. I had my own life to sort out.

At the end of the first week of classes she called and said she wanted to take Maddie and me to lunch the next day. I was disappointed that she asked Maddie too, though it was nice of her. I had so much to talk to her about, I wanted her all to myself. And I wanted to hear what she was doing. But Maddie was pleased, and I was glad my family could do one small thing for her.

When Charlotte arrived, I was so happy to see her, I hardly noticed details, but I was soon aware that Maddie was noticing everything and was impressed. I had already learned something about Maddie that I had never noticed at home — that she was impressed by people's money and belongings. I guess I didn't notice it at home because none of us had anything that would impress her. She was not patronizing or critical of people who did not have material things, but she was awed by people who did have them. It seemed funny to me, when she had so much of her own. Anyway, she looked absolutely bug-eyed over Charlotte's clothes and Charlotte's Porsche (which was Jimmy's) and over the chic little French restaurant in Beverly Hills where Charlotte took us to lunch. And of course my sister played the role to the hilt — big sister, glamour girl, sophisticate, playing kindly hostess to the kids. It was a part she enjoyed, and I enjoyed watching her do it. Part of Charlotte's charm was the sheer pleasure she got from playing the part. She should have been an actress. In a way maybe she was.

After lunch she took us to her apartment, and even I was awed. It was above the Sunset Strip, high up above the city, and it was really grand. She had a sunken living room with an apricot-colored wall-to-wall carpet and white furniture, and two beautiful bedrooms. A real balcony led off the biggest bedroom.

Maddie kept saying, "Super. Oh, Charlotte, it's super. What it must look like at night, with the city all lit up."

Charlotte smiled and said, "It's beautiful, when you can see it."

She's become a real Los Angeleno, I thought, making possessive jokes about the smog. But something struck me as odd about the apartment. There was nothing in it that said "Charlotte" to me. I mean, it could have been any successful woman's decorator apartment. Not a sign of home, not a sign of any of us. But I guess that's what she wanted, a whole new life with none of the past in it. I couldn't help wondering if a person could really accomplish that.

Maddie was full of questions about where Charlotte worked, and all that. Charlotte mentioned a club in Beverly Hills, and then said, "But I free-lance too, you know. And I've cut a few demo records, so we shall see." She looked as if she had no real worries about what she would see.

She took us back to our apartment at three o'clock. Maddie went on talking about Charlotte and her goods and chattels until I really got sick of it. I was pleased that my sister had done so well, but I was worried too. Since she was driving the Porsche, obviously Jimmy was around somewhere, though there had been no sign of him at her apartment, not even shaving things in the bathroom cabinet. I checked. I worry a little about instant success. Or maybe my mother had succeeded in infecting me with her suspicions. I felt uneasy.

Charlotte had not offered to give me her phone number, which was unlisted, but I had read it on her bedroom phone (a beautiful creation of what looked like Delft) and I had memorized it. I didn't intend to use it, but I felt better knowing what it was.

12 ❁ ❁

CHARLOTTE was always in the back of my mind, but I didn't have time to worry or think much about anything except college. It was like coming around the bend of a river in a canoe and suddenly finding yourself in very fast white water. I seemed to be on a dead run from the time I got up in the morning till I collapsed into bed at night.

Things began to shake down. I loved Latin and French, enjoyed American lit after I got used to the professor, who was nervous and young and sarcastic, but I did not like sociology. I saw my advisor and managed to get switched to introductory psychology, which was a lot more interesting.

They all poured on the assignments, and when I wasn't in the library, I was holed up in my room. But that was okay, it was what I was there for. And I really like to study. Maddie didn't seem to be quite as bogged down as I was, but she was always a quick learner. She had begun to make friends, which I'd hardly had time for, though there was a girl in my Latin and French classes that I really liked, a beautiful Japanese girl named Shelley Tanaka. We had lunch together sometimes, or a coffee break, and once in a while we studied together. She had a beautiful lilting voice with what I thought of as a Japanese accent, although it turned out she was born and raised in Hawaii and had never even visited Japan. So much for superficial assumptions.

I didn't hear from Charlotte directly, but about two weeks after I'd seen her, packages began arriving from different stores — Saks, Bullocks Wilshire, Robinson's, Joseph Magnin's — with the greatest clothes, which fit me perfectly. Expensive sweaters, two dresses, skirts, pants, blouses, a camel's hair topcoat, a suede jacket, all brand new, It was pretty overwhelming, especially since the only decent clothes I had with me were the ones she had bought me back home. I wondered if she had felt ashamed of me the day we went to lunch.

Maddie was beside herself, although she had so many gorgeous clothes herself, you wouldn't think she'd even notice anyone else's. "What a terrific sister," she said, when I told her they had to be from Charlotte. "She knows you — you're such a brain, you'd never remember to buy clothes for yourself."

Maddie knew, had to know, that the reason I didn't buy clothes was that I didn't have the money, but I don't think that ever seemed real to her. I myself was getting a little sick of poverty. It was bad enough at home, but here it was painful to say no to dinner at La Grange or a play at the Mark Taper.

I was almost scared to wear those expensive new clothes, and when I did, I felt as if everyone was looking at me, thinking, "Who does she think she is? That little minister's kid, poor as a churchmouse, swishing around in duds from Saks." I had to remind myself that they didn't even know I was the poor minister's kid, existing on loans, grants, and Fleeter charity. Maddie made such a fuss about my going to get a decent haircut that I finally went, though I could not afford fifteen dollars for a haircut that took about fifteen minutes. A dollar a minute. That was more than my professors made. I resisted blandishments for a shampoo and blow dry. I might not be able to cut my hair properly but I could certainly wash it. I had to admit it did look better after it had been "styled," but I went without lunch for a week.

Maddie began to acquire a social life. She went out quite a bit, and on weekends people often gathered at our place. For a while I kept out of it, although Maddie urged me to join them. I stayed in my room and read or studied. Strangers still scared me, and her friends all seemed to have a lot of money. They made me uneasy.

One Saturday night there was a real mob scene in our living room. There must have been twenty people at any one time, though they drifted in and out. They started out barbecuing steaks in the patio, but after a while it got chilly and they began coming in. I got caught in the living room looking for a book, and I couldn't get away. I found myself helping Maddie get out glasses and liquor for the new arrivals, and pretty soon I was trapped. Maddie was unusually excited because Donnie Bridger had come, and she was really carried away by Donnie Bridger. I had to admit he was a handsome guy, and one of those life-of-the-party people, not the boring kind but really amusing. I found myself laughing at him quite a lot, although normally I resist extraverts.

The stereo was on loud, playing disco. A few people were trying without much success to dance in that crowded room. The sofa and the chairs were occupied by couples in various stages of making out. I saw one couple go into my bedroom, thus cutting off my avenue of escape. I was sitting on the floor with a lot of other people jammed together, everybody talking and laughing till you couldn't hear yourself think. Someone was mashed in behind me but all I could see of him was one leg encased in gray tweed.

Donnie Bridger was telling me a long joke, which he kept laughing at as if it were the most uproarious thing he'd ever heard. I couldn't hear enough of it to know, and anyway it made me nervous because I was afraid Maddie would think I was flirting with him. But the more I tried to turn away from him, the more he leaned toward me, talking and laughing.

Suddenly the long gray tweed leg moved, and someone said, "Would you like to get out of this mess and get some fresh air?" A long arm in a white shirtsleeve helped me up, and I saw the rest of my rescuer. He was about five ten, with curly black hair, and he was wearing an unbuttoned sheepskin vest over the white shirt. But the thing that really hit me was an expression in his eyes that reminded me of my twin brother. This person's eyes were gray and Robert's had been blue, but it was the expression, as if he were looking directly at you without any camouflage or any barriers. Very few people look at you that way, even when they know you well.

I followed him across the crowded room, stepping over people, once tripping over someone's feet who by then was too high on pot to notice.

We went down to the patio and sat on the brick wall that surrounded the rose garden. It was suddenly very quiet. The wind had gone down, and although it was cool, it felt good after the heat of the apartment.

"I hate parties," he said.

"I do, too."

He looked at me and smiled. "What were we doing there?"

"I live there."

"Oh. Well, your alibi is better than mine. I got conned into coming by a girl who ditched me thirty minutes after we arrived."

I felt a slight sinking of my stomach. So he had a girl. Well, what of it? I didn't even know him. "Are you brooding?" I was trying to sound light and casual, the way people are supposed to.

He took the question seriously, and thought before he

72

answered. "No, not really. She's kind of a stupid girl actually, only very pretty."

"Oh," I said. I was not stupid and not pretty, so I guessed that left me out of his range of possibilities. Not that I wanted to be anybody's possibility. "What's your name anyway?"

He laughed. "Anyway, my name is Marty Ross. Age twenty. Occupation, pre-med student. Home, Los Angeles. Birthplace, Paris, France. I'm in your Latin class."

"You are?" I was surprised.

"As of today. I got transferred. You wouldn't have noticed, because I am the shy type that sits in the back hoping the professor won't see me."

"Oh. I'm the show-off type that sits in front and answers all the questions."

"You answer a lot of questions, but you're not a show-off. You just happen to be smart."

"And you hate smart women."

"No, no. You've got me wrong. That girl I came with, we wouldn't have lasted long anyway. She's the type that bats her eyes and says, 'Oh, you know so many interesting things.' You know."

I did know. Maddie tended to do that, although Maddie was far from stupid. Somewhere she had got the idea that men liked that. But I knew he wasn't talking about Maddie.

"Are you cold?"

"Not really."

"You're shivering." He took off his sheepskin vest and put it on me. "We can't go back in to that awful party. Why don't we go a movie?"

"All right."

"There's something at the Bruin worth seeing. I don't have my car, so we can't go far. You mind walking?"

"Of course not."

We started down the hill toward Westwood Boulevard.

"How did you happen to be born in Paris, France?" I said.

"My mother happened to be there at the time."

"Are you French?"

"Nope. My mother is from Terre Haute, Indiana. My father was a Hungarian director."

I noticed he said "was" so I thought I'd better not ask questions about his father. I wondered if "director" meant of movies. It could be a funeral director or almost anything. "Do you speak fluent French? *Parlez vous français?*"

"Medium fluent."

"I'm taking French. I've never known any Hungarians. Do you speak Hungarian too?"

"Only a little. It's a nutty language."

"I like languages. I think I'm going to major in languages." I was wondering if he was thinking what a boring conversation this was. He was quiet for several minutes, and I got very nervous trying to think of something brilliant to say.

Finally he said, "Where are you from?"

I told him, and he said, "I've never been to Colorado."

"I've never been to Paris."

He shrugged. "I shook the dust of Paris from my heels some years ago, and I've never looked back."

"My sister lives in Beverly Hills," I said, and then wondered why I said it. I guess because I didn't want him to think I was some kind of hick from the wild West.

But he only said, "Good for her."

It was a good movie. He held my hand. Afterward we had terrific hamburgers and coffee. By the time we got home, the crowd had thinned down, and my room was rumpled but empty. I opened the windows and changed my sheets and went to bed.

Marty Ross had said he would call me, but I never believe that, until it happens.

13 ✿ ✿

A WEEK went by, and I didn't get a call from Marty Ross, though he nodded to me in class. Story of my life. I was having no problems academically, but my social life was about what I'd expected. Maddie and I talked about it one night.

She said, "Sissy, you're ten times prettier than I am, and terrific company. If you just weren't so shy, you'd have guys ringing the phone off the hook."

"Oh, sure."

"I mean it. I've watched guys look at you with that gleam in their eye, and they come over and start talking to you, and you clam up and they go away again."

I sighed. I knew it was true. "I can't think of anything to say. All the brilliant things I think of come to me about six hours later."

"Your self-image is too low."

"My self-image is nonexistent."

"I understand it because I always thought guys wouldn't like me either, but I'm beginning to get over it."

"I should think so. Donnie Bridger is here morning, noon, and night." Maddie really had blossomed out a lot. She had had a permanent that made her blonde hair look fuller, "more body," as the commercials say. And she spent a lot on clothes and wore them well. She has a terrific figure. I'd seen other guys besides Donnie look at her.

She was quiet for a few minutes, and then she said, "How do you feel about sex?"

What a question! "I guess it's here to stay."

"I mean, you were brought up real strict, weren't you?"

"I guess so."

"Well, does it seem terrible to you if a guy has sex with a girl?"

"Oh, come on, Maddie. It's none of my business what people do."

"It wouldn't shock you? Like if Donnie and I . . ."

"Why should it? You like each other a lot. I mean it's your affair, not mine."

"I've never actually done it with anyone. I mean not actually. I've gone right up to that point, but never all the way. Have you?"

"Nope."

"Would you, though, if you really liked a guy?"

"How do I know?" I was thinking about Charlotte. How *did* I know what I'd do? Maybe Jimmy Korvos had some hidden charms, besides money, that I hadn't seen. Maybe she really liked him.

"Well, I just wanted to sound you out. I mean Donnie might stay over some night, and I didn't want you to be shocked." She grinned. "My mother has you here so you'll register shock, you know, keep me on the straight and narrow."

That bothered me. "If that's really true, I ought to move out. I'm not about to be your keeper."

"Oh, Sissy, don't even think of moving out! She'd make me give up the apartment. Anyway there's nobody else I want for a roommate. You and I really get along."

It was true, we did. I was getting really fond of Maddie. There was something honest about her that made her a good friend. You could count on her. "All right, I'll stick around. It is a funny position to be in, though, you know."

"Never kick a gift horse in the teeth." She stretched and got up. "I guess I'll go call Donnie. He was going to the library but he ought to be home by now."

I thought about our conversation. It was true I didn't care what she and Donnie did, and still the effects of my parents' dire warnings about "sin" lingered on enough to make me a little uneasy. I wished she hadn't told me about it, just gone ahead and done what she wanted. I might have suspected, but I wouldn't have *known*. Or maybe I would. The apartment wasn't all that big or soundproof. Oh, the hell with it. I had other problems at the moment. I was trying to find a part-time job, and having no luck. Too many people had the same idea.

The next day Charlotte called, and asked me to go to a dance recital that some friends of hers were giving in a small Hollywood theater.

I always felt proud with Charlotte. She looked so tremendous, and people smiled at her and gave her a lot of attention.

I had never seen professional dancers except on television, and I was really bowled over. The lead dancer, Michael Barski, was incredible. He was so handsome, and in that silver costume that fit him like a second skin he was the sexiest thing I've ever seen. It gave me such a jolt, I almost felt as if I should leave the theater so people wouldn't notice the effect it was having on me. I thought of the conversation Maddie and I had had about sex, and I think for the first time in my life I really understood how a person's scruples and principles could go right out of her head and she could just swoon into a guy's arms and say yes, yes, yes. When I'd calmed down enough to think about it, it was enlightening. It made me understand a lot of people a lot better.

I was more than nervous when we went backstage afterward. It seemed as if everybody must know how I felt about

Michael Barski. It wasn't his good looks or his charm or his intelligence, all of which he had plenty of — it was the feeling of having touched a high-tension wire. When he shook hands with me and smiled, I thought I was going to faint.

He and his friends took us with them to Cantor's restaurant on Fairfax, and I ordered what the others ordered, lox and bagels and hot tea in glasses. Everybody was nice to me, but I was in such a daze, I couldn't do anything but grin like an idiot and nod my head now and then. I hoped Charlotte wasn't ashamed of me. She of course was the life of the party.

Afterward I spent the night at Charlotte's. We went out on the balcony and looked at the city. A wind had driven off the smog, and the city sparkled for miles and miles.

We talked about the dancers, and I tried not to ask too many questions about Michael. I wasn't really terribly interested in information anyway; I just wanted to think about how he looked in that silver suit.

Charlotte asked if I had heard from Mother.

"A couple of times. There's no news. Harvey cries himself to sleep because you and I are both gone."

She looked sad. "Somehow something has to be done about Harvey."

"Like what?"

"He ought to be in school somewhere, so he can develop as far as possible. It's no good, his living at home like that with Mom always hovering over him."

"She'd never let him go."

"I know. He's the baby she can hang onto, the one that won't grow up." She sounded bitter.

"Charlotte, you were the one she loved the most. What's happened? You both sound so bitter."

"Oh, Sis, you know what's happened. She saw me as her second chance. I was to do what she didn't get to do —

graduate from the good college, have a good job for a while, marry the upcoming young executive, live in a Colonial reproduction in the suburbs, have two and a half children . . . And I walked out on the whole bit. She can't forgive me."

"I suppose she feels her life failed her twice. That's kind of sad."

"It's only sad if you can't deal with it. I mean everybody has to adjust. Nothing turns out the way you think it will."

I waited a minute. "Is . . . uh . . . Jimmy still around?"

She gave me a quick glance. "Oh, sure."

"Are you in love with him?"

She laughed. "What an idea." She got up. "Let's go inside. It's getting cool out here. How are you doing at UCLA, Sis?"

"All right. I got a B in a psych quiz."

"Otherwise straight A's?"

"Yes. Maddie got all A's. If she keeps it up, her dad is getting her a Honda Civic for a reward."

"Damn those show-off Fleeters."

"They're really nice though."

She poured herself a shot of bourbon over some ice. "Want some sherry or something?"

"No, thanks."

"Some day I'll get you a Honda Civic. No, damn it, I'll get you a Jaguar."

A little later we went for a quick swim in the pool at the back of the apartment house, being quiet because it was against the rules after midnight. The water was warm, and I felt that strange sensation I always get when I change elements. I had felt it in the plane, and I always felt it in water, not as if I had become a different person but a different species.

When we came back into the apartment, the phone was ringing. Charlotte went into her bedroom to answer it, and closed the door. I went into the other bedroom to get the pajamas Charlotte was lending me, and into the bathroom to take a shower. I was in bed with the light out when she came in. She sat down on the side of my bed.

"Asleep?"

"No. I'm too happy to sleep."

"Remember how Robert used to say, 'Don't let me be too happy; it makes me sick to my stomach'?"

"Yes. I think I remember everything Robert ever said."

She put her hand on my cheek for a second. "It must be really hard, losing a twin. A lot harder than losing a regular brother or sister."

I didn't answer, because there was nothing I could say.

"Sissy," she said, "don't be too idealistic about me, will you. I don't want you to be hurt."

"Idealistic? Is that what I am?"

"I think so. You're a hero-worshipper by nature. But that can hurt an awful lot. I'm just . . . you wouldn't like a lot of things I do. You're kind of a little Puritan, you know."

"I hope I'll get over it."

"Don't get altogether over it. It gives you a solid base, if you know what I mean. I don't have that base, because the way we were brought up made me so sick, I flew off just as far from it as I could get. But you know what your Latin chums say: moderation in all things."

Showing off, I said, "It was a Greek. 'Moderation, the noblest gift of Heaven.' It's in the *Medea,* by Euripides."

She smiled. "Since we're displaying our erudition, how about this?:

> *Others, I am not the first,*
> *Have willed more mischief than they durst:*
> *If in the breathless night I too*
> *Shiver now, 'tis nothing new.*
>
> *More than I, if truth were told,*
> *Have stood and sweated hot and cold,*

80

And through their veins in ice and fire
Fear contended with desire.

Agued once like me were they,
But I like them shall win my way
Lastly to the bed of mould
Where there's neither heat nor cold.

But from my grave across my brow
Plays no wind of healing now,
And fire and ice within me fight
Beneath the suffocating night."

Her voice as she spoke the lines was so low and beautiful, I couldn't speak for a minute. Finally I said, "Your voice is music the way Michael Barski's dancing is music."

She gave a quiet, pleased little laugh, leaned over and kissed me on the forehead. "As an audience of one, my love, you have no equal. But remember what I told you: don't get hurt."

She left, closing my door.

For a long time I lay awake thinking about her. I had never even begun to understand her, and I still didn't. What fire and ice fought within her? Why did she shiver in the night? I had forgotten to ask her who wrote that poem, but the next day she told me it was A. E. Housman.

In the morning after breakfast she drove me back to my place. On the way she asked me if I had a boyfriend.

"Gosh, no. No such luck."

"You will. You just have to learn to relax, don't be off-putting."

"I went to the movies one night with a guy."

"Is he nice?"

"Yeah. Very. He was born in Paris and his father is a Hungarian."

She laughed. "Never trust a Hungarian. But seriously, Sis, if you like him, go after him."

"I don't know how."

"It'll come to you. And listen, if you ever want the Pill, you let me know right away and I'll get them for you."

"The Pill?" I hadn't expected that. I mean that was really rushing things.

"Never get into a stupid kind of jam the way Mom did." She pulled up in front of the house.

"Charlotte, does Mom know you know?"

"Not in so many words. But I'm sure she knows Aunt Pearl and I weren't talking about how cute she was before she had her long curls cut off." She gave me a quick pat. "If you ever have any kind of problem, let me know, all right?"

"All right. And thanks, Charl. For everything."

"We'll do it again soon."

I got out, and vroom vroom, she was gone.

14 ❀ ❀

I COULDN'T get Michael Barski off my mind. I knew it was crazy. It made about as much sense as the time I had a crush on my fifth grade teacher and couldn't sleep. I realized after I finally recovered from Mr. Sanders that it had been because he had liked Robert, and was especially sympathetic and nice to me after Robert died. But Robert had nothing to do with Michael Barski. Twice I went to the ballet again, alone, just to watch him, and the second time I hung around the stage door to get a glimpse of him close up.

He was a long time coming out, and I felt like some kind of stupid groupie. A gaggle of high school girls hung around giggling, and I thought "I'm just as bad as they are."

I really meant to stand far back so he couldn't possibly see me, but he came out all of a sudden and I didn't have time to duck.

He signed autographs for the gigglers, and then he looked at me, perfectly blankly, as if he was waiting for me to ask for his autograph. I felt sick to my stomach. I started to back away and then he suddenly lit up with recognition and said, "Hey, wait! You're Charlotte's little sister."

Little sister. You long for a man to say, "Come to my apartment. I want to make love to you," and he says, "You're the little sister." I gave him a weak grin and tried to think

83

of some excuse for being there. I didn't manage a single word.

Some of the other dancers came out, and he said, "Here's Charlotte's sister."

They said hello politely. I said hello.

"Well, it was nice seeing you," I said.

"Wait a sec," he said. I could see him thinking "Be nice to Charlotte's sister." "You want to join us for coffee?"

I should have said no, thank you, I have to go. Instead I tagged along like some little kid. I was making myself sick.

We went to the same Fairfax Avenue restaurant. They ordered enormous amounts of food and they talked a lot. Now and then they would remember to include me, but mostly not. Michael asked me how school was going. I said, "Fine."

"What are you majoring in?" somebody said.

I said languages.

"Oh, you must take Russian," a girl said, and she went on to tell the others about the year she spent learning Russian. "I wanted to read Pushkin in the original."

"... and Baryshnikov ..." Someone else was having another conversation. "... if I could have seen Nijinsky ..."

I didn't even know who Nijinsky was. I wanted to say to Michael, "Touch me. Just touch me for one second."

"Finnish ..." Someone else was saying. "Finnish is a wild language, nearly all vowels. From the Finno-Ugric ..."

Michael laughed and drank a glass of wine. "Take Finnish, Sissy."

The waiter leaned over the girl next to me with a plate of soup and matzo balls. It smelled wonderful. "Take Yiddish," he said to me, black eyes twinkling.

My head spun. I couldn't follow the conversations. Michael's knee was inches from mine. It was agony to sit there and smile.

At last it was over. A couple from Topanga Canyon

offered me a ride home. Michael said I shouldn't be wandering around alone at night. I knew that. It scared me to death every time I went anywhere, even in daylight. I couldn't say, "I risked my life because I had to see you again." He said good night politely, sent his best to Charlotte, was gone.

It was hard the next day to bring myself back to reality. Shelley Tanaka and I quizzed each other for a test we were having, and I realized I had not studied well enough for it. Shelley was feeling homesick for Hawaii. When the test was over, both of us feeling we really blew it, we got on a bus, more or less on the impulse of the moment, and rode it all the way out Sunset to the beach. It was a foggy, smoggy day, and almost no one was at the beach. We walked a long way, and then bought hamburgers at a little place, and took them back to the beach to eat. It was nice, in spite of the weather. Out here by the sea the smog was not so bad, and the water was warm enough for wading. We wished we had brought swim suits. We waded in until the waves were splashing our rolled-up jeans, and then we ran some more, like a Pepsi commercial, the sand hard and cool under our feet, and seagulls diving and squawking over our heads.

Later Shelley talked a lot about the Big Island. Her family lived in Keaau, a little town between Hilo and the volcanoes. She drew a map for me in the sand.

She told me all about the members of her family, her parents and grandparents and two brothers and a sister. She talked about volcanoes and tsunamis and palm trees and sugar cane fields, surfing and outriggers and Japanese food, banana trees, macadamia groves. . . . I could really see Hawaii for the first time. It had always been a travel poster in my mind.

"Oh, I'd love to go there," I said.

"Sissy, come home with me this summer."

I was so pleased, but of course I couldn't. "I have to

work all summer, or I won't be able to go back to school."

"You could work for my father. You and my father, you'd get along fine, fine."

"What does your father do?"

"He owns a hotel on Banyan Avenue, on the bay. Not big like the Mauna Kea, but a good hotel. Mostly Japanese come there, but he likes to have some haoles too."

"What's haole?"

She giggled. "You. Someone who's not an Islander."

The prospect was so dazzzling, I hardly dared think of it. "What could I do?"

"Oh, anything."

"I've been a waitress and a short-order cook," I said, "in a two-bit cafe in Colorado. That's not much to offer."

"Perfect. You can run a cash register?"

"Sure."

"I'll write to my father today. Okay?"

"Wow," I said. "It's so . . . you better let me think about it."

"Why think? Strike while the iron is hot. Are you worried about your family?"

"No."

"I'll write him tonight."

I ran up and down on the beach till I was exhausted, thinking about Hawaii. Then we talked some more. At last the sun began to go down. We took one last look at the sea, said au revoir to the gulls, and caught a bus for Westwood.

15 ❊ ❊

THINGS were looking up. I had gotten so I could say something besides "hi" to the other kids, when we were hanging around before class or having coffee or whatever. Some of them were friendlier than I had expected. Californians are much more casual than people at home. Of course they always ask about skiing in Colorado, and I have to tell them that where I live, it's flat.

"But you can drive to Vail and those places, can't you?" a girl named Sandy asked me.

"Sure," I said. "If you have a car."

Her eyes widened in surprise and then she laughed. I guess she thought I was joking. It would be hard for a Californian to imagine any human being without a car.

The Fleeters were flying out to take Maddie home for Thanksgiving, and they asked me along, but I had just gotten a part-time job at a bookstore in Westwood. I wasn't sure whether Mom would want me to come anyway, but I'd have liked to see Harvey and everybody. The job was fun, though. I was in the children's department. It was a busy store, especially when people started buying for Christmas, and I enjoyed trying to keep track of all the new books so I could recommend when people asked me to.

Finally, one night when I got home from work, Marty Ross called and asked me to go out to dinner. It was the first real date I'd had since I came to California, not counting going for coffee or a sandwich with somebody. I was excited, and I went into a real dither trying to decide what to wear. Maddie helped me make up my mind finally. I wore one of the dresses that Charlotte had sent me from Robinson's, a light-weight blue wool with a kind of ascot tie.

He took me to a place in Beverly Hills called the Ginger Man. I had cold poached salmon with dill, and Marty had beef Wellington, and we both had enormous salads, and chocolate roll for dessert. It was the best food I ever ate.

For some reason Marty Ross was very easy for me to talk to. I didn't feel that I might say something stupid, the way I felt with most people. He listened seriously to the things I said, as if they mattered, and when I made a joke, his eyes crinkled up in amusement. I really liked him.

"Why do they call you Sissy?" he asked me. We were having black coffee.

"Short for 'Sister.' I've got a brother and four sisters." I paused, wondering whether to tell him about Robert.

"I'm going to call you Sylvia if you don't mind."

"I don't mind. I had a twin brother — he died — he always called me Syl."

He asked about Robert, how he died and everything. He said, "I didn't know anyone died of diphtheria any more."

"They don't, very often. We had a visiting missionary at the time."

"No vaccination?"

"No. My mother thought she didn't believe in all that."

He shook his head. "I'm in pre-med, by the way. Did I tell you?"

I couldn't remember whether he had told me or Maddie, but I knew it. "What kind of doctor will you be?"

"Pediatrician." He said he had been doing a study on twins for psychology, and he asked me questions about what it was like.

88

"When Robert died, it was kind of like having part of myself cut off, literally. I had a lot of trouble adjusting."

"And that's why you're shy."

"I guess." I laughed. "But I'm not acting very shy tonight. People that know me would be amazed, the way I'm telling you my life story."

He smiled.

I told him all about Harvey.

"He ought to be in a school."

"That's what Charlotte says." And then he wanted to know who Charlotte was. I said she was my sister, but I heard myself sounding nervous and evasive, and he tactfully changed the subject.

He had kind of a craggy face, rugged, with strong cheekbones and a square jaw. He smiled more than he laughed, and a lot of the time he looked very serious. His eyes still reminded me of Robert's, the way they looked right at you. I would have expected it to be disconcerting, from someone I hardly knew, but it wasn't.

We drove up the coast afterward. It was a cold, clear night. He parked on a bluff overlooking the ocean. "I'm going to New York after Thanksgiving," he said. "My mother is coming over."

"Over from where?"

"Rome."

"Rome, Italy?"

"Right. After my mad Hungarian papa split, she married an Italian. I guess I didn't tell you, she's an actress."

"A movie actress?"

"Yeah. She's made a few pictures here, but mostly in Italy and France."

"Is she a star?"

"Over there she is."

"My gosh. What's her name?"

"Elena Rossi. I dropped the *i* from my name when I was

a kid. Rossi adopted me, but I wanted to be American, I guess."

"Is Mr. Rossi nice?"

"He's all right. He directs films."

"Gosh, what a glamorous background."

He shrugged. "Backgrounds only seem glamorous to people who aren't in them. Anyway, I'd like you to meet my mother. We're going to have what she calls a week of glorious fun in New York, and then she's coming out here to do a TV film."

"I'd love to meet her." I thought how impressed Charlotte would be. A movie star!

"Actually she's quite nice." He put his arm around me, kind of casually. Then he turned my face toward him and kissed me.

It was really nice. I felt that quick surge of warmth, and I wanted to respond to him, but somehow I got scared and I stiffened up.

He leaned his head back to look at me. "No?"

"Well, I . . ." I couldn't think of anything to say.

"You don't have to be worried. I'm not your average American mad rapist." He sounded offended.

"Oh, I know it." My voice was squeaky.

He took his arm away. "Well, what the hell." He backed up the car and took me home, not saying one word all the way.

At my door I said, "I hope I didn't . . . uh . . . hurt your feelings or anything?"

"No, of course not." He sounded curt. "Do you want to see me again or have I been given the brush?"

"That's silly. Just because I didn't . . . I hardly know you."

"Okay, so I'm overreacting. Do you want to go out Tuesday? It's the night before I go to New York."

So I went out with him Tuesday, and this time we ate at Scandia, on the Strip, and had terrific Scandinavian food.

90

We went down to the Chandler Pavilion to a concert and he held my hand. When he kissed me good night this time, he said, "Are we making headway?"

"Yes," I said, and rushed into the apartment because I wanted to say, "I'll go home with you right now." Good grief! What was the matter with me? Did everybody feel this way, and just have to learn how to deal with it? Or was it just some of us? I knew Maddie felt that way about Donnie. He spent the night quite often now. I guess my mother must have felt that way about whoever got her pregnant. Was that how Charlotte felt too? About Jimmy? No, not from what she had said. In the bookstore I had looked through a book called *Sex and the Teenage Girl,* when nobody was looking. I was almost eighteen and I didn't think of myself as a teenager, but I thought there might be something I had missed. It didn't really tell me anything useful, though, nothing I didn't already know. I didn't need menstruation explained to me, for heaven's sake, nor the dangers of venereal disease, or the statistics about unwed teenage mothers. I wanted to know what you do when your body tells you it wants somebody but the principles you grew up with tell you to restrain your desires. Something inside my head told me that falling into bed with every Tom, Dick, and Harry who came along was definitely not what I wanted to do. But how could you be sure when a guy was not in that class, when he was really somebody special?

Well, the question had not arisen yet, with Marty. But I had a feeling it would before long.

16 ❋ ❋

THE phone rang. I hate telephones, and I always put off answering till the third or fourth ring. Then if they've hung up, I worry about who it was. It was Marty calling from New York, and I was glad I had answered in time. It was wonderful to hear his voice. He always sounds so sane.

He said he was having a ball. He and his mother were at the St. Regis, and they had been to a play every single night.

"How is she?" It was hard to imagine this glamorous parent.

"Great. Still got her sense of humor. Listen, we're getting in Saturday night, and she'll be at the Beverly Hills for a few days before I drive her to La Jolla, where they're making the film. Could you have dinner with us Sunday?"

"I'd love to."

"Good. I'll call you after we get in. Bye, love."

I had never known anyone who stayed at the Beverly Hills. I had never been called "love" before.

After he hung up, I went into the bedroom and wrapped the "Fidelio" album I had bought for Harvey, and the box of Coachella dates I was sending my parents. I felt good. I turned on Maddie's multiband radio and listened to some good Christmas music from England and Holland.

I had explained to Mom that I couldn't come home for Christmas, mainly because of my job at the bookstore, but also because I didn't have the money. The Fleeters were going to take Maddie to Acapulco for Christmas break, and Shelley Tanaka was going to Hilo. She had promised to remind her father about a summer job for me.

With everyone going away, I had expected to be lonesome over the break, but now I forgot all about that. There were Marty and his mother and the Beverly Hills Hotel and all that magic coming up. I hadn't heard from Charlotte for ages, but maybe if she wasn't going anywhere, we could get together over the holidays. I was feeling very good.

Sunday came finally.

He was right on time. I'd never seen him dressed up before, and I must say, he looked great. He said *I* looked great, so there we went, two great-looking people catching a casual snack at the Polo Lounge.

He left me in the lobby while he went to get his mother. It took a little while, and although I tried to play the game of movie-star searching, I was getting really nervous. I'd just spotted Doris Day (I *think* it was Doris Day), when I saw Marty and his mother coming toward me. She was so beautiful, I forgot all about Doris Day. Marty's mother was gorgeous. She looked a little like Ava Gardner on the late show, and she moved like a dancer. She was talking and smiling and holding Marty's arm, and he was smiling at her in a pleased kind of way. I guess anybody would be pleased to have a mother that looked like that. People turned to look at her, and a couple stopped her, embraced her, and chatted. Marty looked at me and made a little gesture of impatience. Then, since his mother kept on talking to the people, he came and took me by the hand and led me to her.

She turned to look at me with a really warm smile, and said, "You're Sylvia," and introduced me to the couple as her son's friend.

When they left, Marty said, "Mother, let's go in to dinner before anybody else discovers you." He winked at me and said, "It's like trying to walk through Piccadilly Circus with Queen Elizabeth."

"Darling, how you exaggerate." She put her hand on my arm and let Marty guide us to the Polo Lounge. "I'm so glad to meet you," she said to me. "Marty talks about you a great deal." She had a very slight accent that was not Indiana. I supposed she must have picked it up, living in Europe. It was attractive.

She charmed the maître d', who called her Signorina Rossi, and she charmed the waiter and the wine man and the busboy and a good many other people who just looked at her as she walked by. I myself was so overcome, I had so far not said a word except "How do you do."

Marty recommended what I should order, and I nodded. I was too excited even to read the menu. It was just a big blur.

Elena Rossi talked a lot, in a beautiful, low-pitched voice. She was funny, witty, and she didn't seem to mind that I didn't say anything brilliant in reply — or much of anything at all. She did not say, "How quiet you are," or "How shy you are," or as they used to say when I was younger, "Cat got your tongue?" remarks that always rendered me totally speechless and ashamed. Instead she talked as if I had answered. Marty said things now and then, but mostly he too just listened, smiling in a pleased sort of way, and looking from one to the other of us. I was impressed with his poise, the way he handled waiters, the easy way he sat there. Maybe having a mother like Elena does that for you, although I can see it could have the opposite effect.

I think the dinner was very good, although I don't remember too much about it. By the time we reached the entree, I had begun to speak now and then. Elena listened attentively to everything I said, and the more she did that, the more at ease I felt. Pretty soon I was talking like an almost normal human being.

She told us funny stories about Europe, about her films, about Italian workmen, about the villa she was having remodeled. I told her I wanted to take Italian next year.

"She's majoring in languages," Marty said. "She's terrific in Latin class. She's a super-brain."

I was embarrassed but pleased. I didn't know he thought I was smart.

She sipped her wine and studied me a minute. "One hears so much about what a miserable lot your generation is. I think that's insane. I think young people were never so bright, so aware, so interested in a wide range of things. You must come visit me in Italy, Sylvia."

"The young have had a bad press," Marty said. "The age of instant gratification, and all that jazz is mostly invented by middle-aged people." He and Elena discussed gratification for a minute, but I was thinking about Italy. Rome. Florence. Venice.

"A cultured human being," Elena was saying, "is one who keeps a tight rein, who stays in the driver's seat, and lives by concepts larger than himself."

I was thinking of Charlotte saying to me, "I've got a handle on life now. I can swing it around my head like a discus," and I remembered thinking, "But what happens when you let go?"

I missed a bit in the conversation, trying to get my elbows out of the way of the waiter taking away the dessert plates and bringing coffee and cointreau. When I caught up, Marty was talking about a drug called phencyclidine. "Otherwise known as angel dust. They use it to tranquilize grizzly bears. You can make it easy as anything in a chemistry lab. A guy I know uses it to doctor his marijuana. One of these days he's going to go right 'round the bend and stay there."

I thought of the music teacher we had in the eighth grade. Mr. Luscomb. He'd been a concert violinist, but something happened — the rumor was he'd gotten hooked on drugs. But he taught me more about music than I'd ever learned in my life. For a moment I saw him vividly in my mind, silently conducting the recording of the Schubert Unfinished that was playing on the stereo. His eyes shut, head thrown back, arms waving up and down. The other kids laughed at him, but for the rest of my life I'll know the Unfinished as intimately as I know my own face. He hated us all, I'm sure, hated teaching. In the middle of the year he OD'd and died in his old Chevrolet in a field outside of town, Suicide, they said. I closed my eyes and thought, "God, give Mr. Luscomb a violin."

"Are you all right?" Marty said.

"Oh. Sure. I've never been more all right."

He smiled and relaxed. It was strange that I should sit there with tears stinging my eyes over Mr. Luscomb, five years dead, when this was the most exciting night of my life.

They were talking about a cousin of theirs, who was on drugs. That was what had brought the subject up. I put the pieces of the conversation back together.

"Poor Myra," Elena said. "One does what one can for her, but there isn't much you can do. She has a fatal fondness for unsavory characters."

We sat a little while longer over our coffee. A distinguished-looking man with white hair paused near our table, peered at Elena, and came up to her. "Elena, is it really you?" He had a strong French accent.

"Jean! How marvelous to see you. I didn't know you were over here." She lapsed into French, and they talked animatedly for a few minutes, mostly too fast for me to understand. She introduced him to us, and after he left, she watched him for a moment and then said, "That, my darlings, is one of the three best directors in France."

Marty laughed and leaned over and kissed her. "Baby,

you've come a long way from Terre Haute." He called the waiter for the check.

Elena went out ahead of us, seeing someone else she knew and wanted to speak to. I stood near the table waiting for Marty. I glanced around the room and suddenly at a table for two not far from me, I saw my sister Charlotte. The man she was with was tall and bald but he was back to me, and I couldn't see his face.

I said, "Charlotte!" and took a step toward her .

She looked up and saw me and something like fear flashed in her eyes. She gave a little shake of her head and frowned and turned her head away. I was stunned.

"What is it?" Marty was at my side.

I couldn't speak for a minute. Then I said, "Oh, nothing. I thought I saw someone I knew. . . ." I walked past her table and out of the room.

If I could have done it, I'd have walked right on out of the hotel and into the night. But there were thank yous and good-byes to be said, the right things to be spoken of. On the way home Marty was nearly as silent as I was. Finally, he said, "Did you like her?"

"Your mother?"

"Who else?"

"I've never met anyone I liked more."

At my door he said, "In the restaurant you said, 'Charlotte.' Did you see your sister?"

I tried to laugh but it came out like a croak. "Oh, no. I thought for a minute . . ." I choked on tears. I got the door unlocked and went in, hoping he hadn't noticed.

17 ❋ ❋

MARTY called me in the morning to say they were leaving for La Jolla and to wish me a happy Christmas.

"Don't be lonesome."

"I won't." I tried to tell him how much I had enjoyed the evening; I'd done such a miserable job of thanking him the night before.

"Elena thinks you're terrific. Listen, I'll call you as soon as I get back, okay? Probably in two or three days."

As soon as I had hung up, the phone rang again. It was Charlotte, sounding worried. "Sissy?"

I felt myself freeze.

"Sissy, I want to explain about last night."

"No need to."

"Of course there's a need to. I can't tell you much about it over the phone, but I wasn't just out with a guy. We were discussing something very important."

"Sure."

She began to sound angry. "Sissy, stop sounding like that."

"Like what?"

"Like a frozen cod. I could not talk to you last night. I could not have talked to anyone . . . I could not have talked to God himself."

"So all right. What's the big deal?"

"The big deal is that you're mad."

"Look, Charlotte, I have to get ready for work. Some other time, all right?" I hung up. I hung up on Charlotte. The phone rang again, for a long time, but I didn't answer it. I went to work feeling awful.

By the end of the day I was thoroughly ashamed of myself, and willing to admit that Charlotte probably did have a good reason for not speaking to me. She had never snubbed me before. All the way home I kept being reminded that it was Christmas Eve. The stores blazed with lights, the Salvation Army man rang his bell, people smiled and said, "Merry Christmas" to each other, people passed me carrying wrapped packages. I had not dreamed I would feel so homesick.

As soon as I got home, I tried to call Charlotte, but her phone was busy. When I tried again, she didn't answer. I had bought her a present at the bookstore — a gift-box set of *The Bell Jar* and *Ariel*. She liked Sylvia Plath.

I wrapped it up and right after I'd eaten, I caught a Sunset bus and got off at the corner of Sunset Plaza Drive. It is a steep climb up the hill, and I was really puffing by the time I got to Charlotte's. I went slowly up the stairs to her landing, and just before I reached the top of the stairs, I stopped for a minute to get my breathing under control. I hoped she wouldn't be out, but if she was, I could leave the package up against her door. All the apartments had separate landings and stairs so nobody would be likely to steal it.

I heard Charlotte's door open and I heard her voice, although from where I stood, I couldn't see her.

"Thanks for coming, Doug," she said.

A man's voice laughed. *"Not* Doug, baby. Dave."

She laughed. "Sorry about that."

"You must have a good client, name of Doug."

"Dave, you're going to like the stuff. It's really super."

"If it's as good as you are, honey . . ."

She said something, but her voice was muffled. I felt frozen stiff. I tried to turn around and go downstairs, but I couldn't move. I hung onto the banister as if I were in danger of falling.

I heard the man say good-bye, heard him start down the stairs. It was too late to get away from there. He was about forty years old, in an expensive-looking suit with the jacket slung over his shoulder. He had a small package in his hand, and when he saw me, he shoved it into the pocket of his jacket, gave me a sharp look, and hurried past.

I got to the top of the stairs just as Charlotte was closing the door. She hadn't seen me. I grabbed the door handle and shoved. It flew open and almost hit her. She was wearing a long white terrycloth bathrobe and she was barefoot. She had a thick wad of money in her hand.

"Sissy!" She looked frightened.

I went in and slammed the door. "I brought your Christmas present. I seem to have come at a bad time." I threw it at the sofa; it missed and fell on the floor.

She picked it up, still staring at me. "You should have called first." She stuffed the money into her robe pocket.

"Obviously." My head was pounding and my ears rang, as if somebody had given me a hard wallop on the side of the head.

"Well, I'm sorry, but I don't have to apologize to you or anybody else for the way I live."

"How long have you been a prostitute?"

She winced. "That's a nasty way to put it."

"How do *you* put it?"

She gave a little laugh. "I guess I think of myself as a very high-priced and exclusive call-girl."

"And drug-pusher."

"There are worse ways of making a living."

"Name one." I was shaking all over, and I had this terri-

101

ble feeling that I was going to hit her. The awful thing was, she looked just the way she always looked. She looked like the Charlotte I had loved and looked up to all my life. On the outside nothing had changed.

"Now look, Sissy." She stuck her hands into her pockets and she was beginning to be angry. "I'm sorry you found out, but it's none of your damned business actually. I make my own decisions, I live my own life. I have my reasons for what I'm doing."

"I always thought you were perfect. You were my ideal . . ." I had to stop because my voice broke.

"I never asked for that. It's goddamned uncomfortable, if you want to know, having somebody see you like that. All the time I'm thinking how shocked you're going to be when you find out I'm not some kind of paragon. I'm a human being like everybody else."

"I don't know any other human beings that do what you're doing."

"That's because all you know is Fort Lewis, Colorado, and only one limited part of that. Don't come on all self-righteous with me, Sissy. You sound too much like Mom, and we know what all that great morality act amounts to. It's all a bunch of hypocritical shit. I don't intend to live that kind of life."

"You had all the breaks."

She interrupted. "Oh, sure. I got into a good college, and Mom takes the credit for that. It was *my* grades got me in, not hers; it was *my* damned hard work when I was in high school. I'm not as smart as you; I had to work for my grades, but I got them. So I'm supposed to drag through four years of college, wearing secondhand clothes and never having a dime to spend, and for what? So I can teach in some fucking inner-city school somewhere, or some rotten little town like Fort Lewis? Marry a nice little bank teller? A supermarket manager? Thanks a lot, but no, thanks. I

102

intend to enjoy life, and you can't do that without money. I learned that the hard way, and so did you. All right, so I am using the only talent I have — a body that attracts men, a body men will pay high for."

"Is Jimmy your pimp?"

"You do like the ugly words, don't you? Of course he is. And to tell you God's truth, I'm getting sick of laying out a big cut of what I make to him. That's why I'm dealing. He doesn't know a thing about that. This is *my* business. I can really clean up in about a year, and then I'll be free, free of everybody, my own boss."

"I remember when you were county fair queen. You were on television. You had a gold crown. . . ."

"Made of cardboard. Oh, Sissy. Try to understand, won't you? I can't bear it to fight with you. Look, I'm still your Charlotte. I love you."

"You're a lousy whore."

She gasped and then she hit me, a hard slap in the face. Then she began to cry. I turned around and ran out of there.

It was dark outside and I could taste the smog. I walked fast down the hill and turned right on the Strip. There were no people on the sidewalk, but cars went by, lights on, driving fast, each car a contained world. None of it had anything to do with me.

I walked without thinking where I was going, just wanting to keep moving, trying not to think. My cheek stung from the slap. Maybe if I walked hard enough and far enough, it would all begin to fade, the way a bad dream goes after you've been awake a while.

I finally became aware that a car was driving along beside me, close to the curb. The driver kept leaning toward the passenger side and saying something to me. All at once I was terrified. Ordinarily I'd just have turned a corner or crossed the street. It wasn't as if the street were deserted, after all. But I was cold with fear. I tried to walk faster, and he speeded up. A car blew its horn at him and passed him. I came to a stoplight. Of course. All I had to do was to cross the street and walk on the other side.

While I waited for the light, he opened the passenger door and said something. I heard him this time, and what he said made me want to throw up. As the light changed, I ran out into the intersection, but I had to wait in the middle of the street for a woman making a right turn. While I waited, the man made a left turn, so that when I got across Sunset and started across the intersecting street, he was blocking me. I thought literally that I was going to die, that all kinds of horrible sexual acts were going to be performed on me and that then I would be slowly and painfully killed.

Just then the car suddenly started up and sped off down the hill. I couldn't believe it. He was gone! Then I saw why. A patrol car came around the corner and stopped. A young cop got out and came over to me. His voice was pleasant, but he was looking at me very closely.

"Having a little trouble?"

"He was trying to pick me up. He . . ." To my horror I began to cry.

"Well, he's gone. But you shouldn't be wandering around here after dark by yourself. Where do you live?"

"Westwood."

"What were you doing over here?"

"I just . . . I just took a Christmas present to my sister."

"Well, why don't you get in the car and we'll run you home." He held the door open.

Under the light from the dome he took my driver's license and wrote down my name and address. "Fort Lewis, Colorado." He looked at his partner. "You going to school?"

"Yes. UCLA." I was trying to stop the stupid tears.

"I guess the big city can get kind of scary. But no need to cry, miss. You're all right now."

104

When we got to the apartment, he walked me up to the door. "Just don't wander around L.A. by yourself after dark. There's too many kooks around."

"Yes. Thanks." I couldn't seem to get the key in the lock. He took it and opened the door for me.

"There you are. Lock your door now."

"I will."

"Merry Christmas."

I went upstairs and threw myself on my bed. I didn't even take off my coat or my shoes. I stayed there like that all night. I could hear somebody's radio playing Christmas carols.

18 ❀❀

WHEN I woke up, the sun was streaming in and I couldn't remember for a minute why I was in bed with my clothes on. Sometime during the night I must have taken off my coat, because it was on the floor, but I still had my shoes on. I sat up and remembered. I lay down again. It was Christmas Day. There didn't seem any point in getting up.

After a while I decided I had to have a long hot shower and I had to wash my hair. I stayed in the shower for ages, soaping myself all over, again and again, scrubbing myself with the loofah till my skin tingled. Then I brushed my teeth, got a big glass of orange juice, put on my bathrobe, and went back to bed. I felt weak and dizzy.

I kept seeing Charlotte in my mind and then driving the image out, almost by force. I slept again. When I woke up, I could hear people talking out on the patio. They had a radio going. A minister's voice came on, right after some organ music. His voice reverberated, as if he were in a big church somewhere. He was saying, ". . . and the blessed baby Jesus lay in his manger, and all around the angels sang. . . ." Somebody on the patio said, "Oh, Christ," and flipped the dial to a rock station. They laughed.

I decided I had to think about last night. I couldn't lie here forever fighting it off. I went over the whole scene in my mind. Part of the pain was that I couldn't understand it. I just couldn't see how she could let herself be used, as if she were some kind of public utility. I thought about a guy named Tim McClaren, Don McClaren's brother, the only guy I ever knew about that she was in love with. He was older, by four or five years, and Mom raised hell about Charlotte's going out with him. There was a terrible scene when Mom asked him a lot of humiliating questions about his intentions. He left town soon after that, and as far as I knew, Charlotte had never seen him again. I remembered how she had cried, late at night when she thought I was asleep. And the look on her face when Mom told her it was for her own good. Charlotte must have been about sixteen then.

Maybe I should have talked to her, tried to comfort her. But I was scared when she cried like that. I was only a kid. I had never mentioned Tim to her. Maybe what she was doing now was some kind of revenge. Once, just recently, she had laughed and said, "You know the saying, Sissy. 'Living well is the best revenge.' "

I knew I ought to get up and eat something, but I didn't feel like it. I was just thirsty. I brought a whole pitcher of orange juice into the bedroom, and a box of saltines in case I got hungry. I felt sick to my stomach and dizzy, and it was hard to move, as if my arms and legs suddenly weighed a thousand pounds. I drank some juice and went to sleep again.

The phone rang and went on ringing. Half an hour or so later it rang again. Finally I got up and put some pillows over it. When it was getting dark, it rang again, and somebody rang the doorbell a long time. I heard a car drive away. I wasn't even curious about who it was.

I slept hard all night and woke up with a headache. I made myself call the bookstore to tell them I didn't feel well and wouldn't be in.

108

Mrs. Mitchell said, "Do you need anything, Sissy? Are you there alone? Your voice sounds strange."

"I'm all right, thanks."

"Call me if you need anything. And don't come in till you feel up to it. There won't be much business now."

I went back to sleep. Every once in a while through the day the phone whirred under the pillows. I ate some saltines and drank some more juice but it was warm now and didn't taste too fresh. I switched to water. My throat felt tight. I slept and slept.

In the middle of the night I got a glass of milk from the refrigerator, but I could only drink half of it. In the morning the phone began again. I hoped it wasn't Marty. I could imagine how he would feel about me if he knew my sister was a call girl. And how shocked his mother would be. She supposedly thought I was such a nice girl. And the Fleeters! They'd throw me out right away. I was going to have to go anyway. It wasn't right to go on living off the Fleeters. But I couldn't make any decisions or do anything now. Maybe when I felt better, I'd just go home. Mom would not be pleased, but it was my home. Where else could I go?

The next day, I think it was afternoon, though my little clock had run down and my watch too, and I'd lost track of time — I heard the doorbell ringing and ringing, and somebody knocking. I put the pillow over my ears.

Pretty soon I heard the front door open and close.

"You okay, Miss?" It was the manager, with Marty right behind him.

"Yes."

"All right to let this guy in?"

"Yes. Thank you. I was asleep."

He gave me a searching look and left.

"For God's sake, Sylvia," Marty said. "Are you all right?" He looked pale and scared.

"I'm all right."

He came over closer to me, frowning down at me worriedly. "You're white as a sheet. Why are you in bed? Why haven't you answered the phone or the door? Jesus, I've been going out of my mind."

I tried to sit up, but the room spun and I had to shut my eyes and duck my head. He was sitting on the bed holding me.

"Easy, now. Easy. Keep your head down."

I remember I thought what a good doctor he'd be; he was so gentle and reassuring. I wanted to cry, but I didn't have the energy to cry.

"When did you eat last?"

I couldn't remember. "I'm not hungry."

After he got me settled back in bed, he went into the kitchen and was gone a little while. He came back with tea and a bowl of milk toast, "graveyard stew," Charlotte always called it, and after he got me sitting up, he fed me the milk toast, slow spoonfuls, giving me time in between to make sure I could keep it down. Then I drank the tea. I did feel a little better.

He put his hand on my forehead. "No fever. Does your throat hurt?"

"It just feels tight."

He studied me. "Has anything happened? Are you upset about anything?"

I looked away and didn't answer.

"Incidentally, you have some flowers. The florist truck came while I was pounding on your door." He got up and came back a few minutes later with a dozen long-stemmed yellow roses in one of Maddie's vases. He put them on the bureau. "There's a card. Shall I read it to you?"

I didn't care. It was probably a mistake, probably they were meant for Maddie.

He opened the card. "It says, 'Forgive me. I love you. Charlotte.'"

I turned over with my face to the wall so he wouldn't see the pain. I thought of the terrible things I had said to her. No matter what she had done, I had no right to treat her like that. I ought to do something. Call her or something. But I was too tired. I went to sleep.

It was evening when I awoke. Marty was sitting in a wicker chair that he had brought from the living room, reading, with just the small lamp on.

"You'll ruin your eyes," I said.

He put the book down at once and came over to me. "That's the first voluntary thing you've said since I got here. Do you feel any better?"

"I think so." I tried to sit up but right away I got very dizzy and had to lie down again. "I don't know what's the matter with me."

"Do you think you should see a doctor?"

"No, I'm not sick."

"But Syl, you certainly aren't well."

"I just don't feel like doing anything. It will go away."

He was holding my hand. "Is it depression?"

"Depression?" The very word made me feel tired. I closed my eyes.

"Something has happened."

I began to cry. I wasn't making any sound, but I couldn't stop the tears that dripped down my face. He took off his shoes and lay down on the bed, holding me in his arms. I cried harder.

I said, "Don't leave me."

"I won't leave you, love." He stroked my hair and held me so close I could feel his heart beat. I cried till my head was splitting and my nose was running. He found some Kleenex in my bathrobe pocket. He slipped his hand under my robe and stroked my shoulder. He kissed my face and my hair. He felt as tense as a spring.

All that night whenever I woke up, he was awake and

111

holding me in his arms. He got me some fresh orange juice once, and toward dawn he made me an eggnog but I couldn't drink it all.

In the morning he made breakfast, just juice and tea and toast with marmalade. It seemed as if quite a lot of time went by, but he never left me.

"Don't you have to be somewhere?" I asked him once.

"Priority is here."

That night, after the lights were out and he was holding me, I told him about Charlotte. He was quiet for a long time, and I thought, "This is the end. I won't see him anymore."

Finally in a very gentle voice he said, "Poor Syl. Poor baby." He kissed me gently. "What a jolt."

"So I'll probably be going home soon. But I want you to know I appreciate . . ." I began to cry again.

"Go home? What for?"

I hadn't thought about why I felt I had to go home. I didn't want to have to think about it. "It seems obvious."

"Not to me. Nor to you either, I'll bet. You're just wanting home because you've been hurt. You want your mother."

"My mother is the last one I'd run to."

He was silent for a minute. "Poor old Charlotte," he said.

"Poor *Charlotte?*"

"She must be suffering too. Those flowers, that note . . . She was real fond of you, right?"

"I thought so."

"And she knew you looked up to her as if she were some kind of goddess. She must have dreaded the day you'd find out."

It was what Charlotte had said herself. "She's a prostitute."

"I know, you keep saying that. And it's not socially acceptable, is it? But I suppose everybody has or thinks he has some reason for what he does."

112

"She must be a nymphomaniac."

"I wouldn't think so. From what I've heard and read about prostitutes, they usually aren't interested in sex. That's why they can treat it like something unimportant; it doesn't mean anything to them."

"She deals in drugs."

"I wish she didn't do that; that's dangerous. In this town especially, you don't tread on other people's territory in a racket as profitable as drugs." He was quiet for a few minutes.

I tried to imagine what he was thinking.

"Why don't you try to get a little sleep now," he said.

"It's all I've done is sleep."

"I know, but it's good for you right now."

I didn't think I could sleep anymore, but I did, feeling almost safe in his arms.

19 ❊ ❊

MARTY coaxed me into going into the living room and sitting in the big chair in the sunshine. He put the Mahler Fourth on the stereo.

"Listen," he said, "I have to go home for a few minutes. . . ." I guess I looked scared, because he said, "I'll be right back. You just stay put." He held my hand to his cheek so I could feel the roughness. "If I don't get a shave pretty soon, I'll be picked up for vagrancy. You either have to have an honest-to-God beard or shave; there's no middle ground in this cruel world." He kissed my fingers. "Also I need some clean clothes. What do you feel like eating? How is your stomach?"

"It's all right now."

"Name your favorite food in all the world, price no object."

I couldn't believe I felt good enough to make a joke. "A foot-long chili dog."

"Pretty exotic, but I'll see what I can do."

I hated having him gone, but the sun was warm and the chair was comfortable. I thought about calling Charlotte to thank her for the flowers, but I couldn't seem to do it. When I thought of the phone ringing in that apartment, I had an instant image of some john in there with her. I could write her a note . . . but I didn't do anything.

I was asleep when Marty came back. And he did have a foot-long chili dog, two of them, and some groceries, his Doppkit, clean shirts and socks and shorts and a bathrobe.

"Looks like I'm moving in," he said, "and I never thought to ask if it's all right."

"You know it is. Right now I . . ." I bit into the chili dog. "This is wonderful. Right now I don't want to be alone."

"Understood. You have chili on your chin." He got me a paper napkin.

He had brought his books too, and while I half-slept, half-watched him, he sat on the floor and pored over an anatomy book.

He fixed a wonderful dinner. I was beginning to be terribly hungry, and he said it was a good sign.

"I was thinking I should take you to this doctor I know, he's a great guy, and he could give you a prescription for an antidepressant. There's no sense suffering with it when you don't have to."

"No, I don't want any pills. I can beat it myself."

He nodded approvingly. "I think so. You're a gutsy one."

"That's not true, though. I've always been somebody's shadow."

"That may have been true once, but it isn't now."

I didn't really want to think about it, and he didn't press it. I just sat there, listening to the stereo, noticing the way Marty's hair curled and how long his eyelashes were, and that rugged jaw all shaved now. I'd have to be careful not to get dependent on him. Having him around was habit-forming. I closed my eyes and pretended nothing bad had happened.

The next day he asked if it was okay to use the phone to call his mother. I sent him into Maddie's room so he could have some privacy. When he came back, he said, "Got an idea for you."

"What?"

"My mother is going on location. She offered me the

house for a few days. Want to go? La Jolla is nice if it isn't foggy."

"She might not want you to bring me."

"She suggested it." He read what I was thinking. "I guess my mother and yours probably react differently to things."

"I'd have to take off from my job."

"This is Friday. If we had to, we could come back Monday. Why don't you call your boss?"

I didn't know what I thought about it. I wanted to go, but it seemed like some kind of important step, and I wasn't sure I wanted to take it. But I called the bookstore.

Mrs. Mitchell was great. She said I might as well take off till the new semester started. "It's dead here. But don't forget to come back, Sylvia. You're one of the best I've ever had."

That cheered me up a good deal. Still I hesitated. I just didn't feel up to anything.

"I'll pack for you," Marty said. "And look, it's not a seduction plot, honest. I'll admit I'd like nothing better than to seduce you (what a word! It sounds like an old movie), but you've got enough stuff to straighten out in your head now without that. I wouldn't want it to turn into a guilt trip. When you let me make love to you, and note I said 'when,' not 'if,' I want it to be right and happy for you. Okay?"

I looked at him a few seconds and then I held out my hand. "I like you, you know that?"

He grinned. "I'm a modest type. I never would have guessed."

"Well, I do."

He made me sit on the bed and tell him what to pack. And finally we came out of the house and got into his VW. It seemed to me as if I had not been out of the house for months.

"La Jolla," he said, "here we come."

117

20 ❀ ❀

D R. Seuss lives on that hill over there," Marty said. We were lying on pads beside the swimming pool in back of the house his mother had rented. It was a beautiful little house, on a hill overlooking the harbor. The sun was out, and the air was so clear and clean, we both kept taking long breaths just to enjoy it.

"Dr. Seuss? You're kidding."

"No, really."

I was lying on my stomach, and he was rubbing suntan oil into my shoulders and back. I was wearing one of his mother's swim suits, a bikini, and I was thinking, "The minister's kid from Fort Lewis is lying beside a pool in a bikini. Borrowed, of course." I laughed, and he asked me what I was thinking.

I told him, and he gave me a long thoughtful look.

"Tomorrow we go downtown and you buy yourself a swimsuit. With *your* money."

"Umm. Trying to make me throw my money away." His hands on my back and the warm sun were relaxing me almost to sleep.

"It's a symbol. Sylvia's flag of liberation. You have a nice back."

"Thank you." A few minutes later I said, "My father bought a Dr. Seuss book for Robert and me once. He used to read it to us."

119

"What kind of guy is your father?"

"It's hard to say. He used to seem one way, now he seems another." I tried to explain how he withdrew from us after Robert died. "I suppose he's weak."

"Maybe not. If he really though he'd done badly as a parent, I could see how he might move away from that area into his parish, where he knew he did a good job."

"We're big on guilt in our family."

"You know what I think about you? — Hey, this makes me feel very sexy, stroking your back and legs like this. Do you mind?"

"No." It made me feel sexy too, but in a warm, slow way. "What do you think about me?"

"I think you have taken on everybody's guilt. Your father's, your mother's, your own because Robert died and you lived, and now Charlotte's."

"I don't think Charlotte feels any guilt."

"But you do, on her account. Tell you what I want you to do. I want you to say to yourself twenty-five times a day, 'I am Sylvia, and nobody else. I am responsible for Sylvia, and nobody else.' "

"I am Sylvia," I said drowsily. "What kind of little boy were you? I was thinking about it last night."

"Were you? That's a good sign. Well, I was a very confused little boy."

"Tell me."

"First five years in Budapest, of which I have only hazy memories. We lived in a big old-fashioned apartment with high ceilings and carved fireplaces, on the fifth floor of an old place that looked like Paris. It had an elevator but the elevator man was the neighborhood Communist, and he only ran the elevator when he wasn't at a meeting or something, so you had to climb all those outside iron steps, and I'd get scared, looking down into the courtyard. The landlady's husband had been shot by the Russians, and she used to cry a lot at night. I could hear her. Then my mother and father broke up. I was just as glad. He used to yell at me a lot in Hungarian, and then he'd have fits of remorse and kiss me, and his moustache tickled."

I turned over to look at him. "Is this for real?"

"Sure. We lived in Paris a few years, I started school, and then my mother met Rossi and we lived in Rome and sometimes Paris, sometimes London, sometimes Hollywood. Rossi had never had kids, and he didn't know what to do with me. They broke up a couple of times on account of me. Then he adopted a policy of pretending I didn't exist. My mother and I were always friends, but she was working a lot. When I was old enough, they sent me to school in Switzerland. Then she brought me over here and enrolled me at Harvard — the Episcopal boys' school in the Valley."

"And you didn't know anybody."

"No. It took me the whole four years to get adjusted. The other guys thought I was some kind of faggot because I spoke English with an accent, and I knew how to play rugby but not football or baseball."

"You don't have an accent now."

"I got rid of it as fast as I could." He grinned. "So there's the story of my life. If I get into a pickup baseball game now, I can take care of myself. But if somebody screamed at me in Hungarian, I'd probably wet my pants."

I thought about it. He had had a lot more to cope with than I had ever had. I felt ashamed of myself for being such an egocentric baby. I said so, and he said, "Oh, great God, don't go laying a guilt trip on yourself on my account. That's what we're trying to cure." He jumped up. "Race you six laps." And he dove into the pool.

That night we drove into San Diego and had dinner at Mr. A's.

When we got back to the house, I said, "I'm going to call Charlotte."

121

"Good," he said. "I was hoping you would."

I went into his mother's bedroom, where the phone was. It was a pretty room, very feminine, and it smelled good. For a moment I couldn't remember Charlotte's number. Then it came to me. I dialed and listened to the phone ringing in her apartment. My hands were wet. I almost hung up. It rang and rang, and I began to feel frightened for no reason at all.

Then someone, a man, said, "Hello, hello?" in an angry, impatient voice.

I thought I might have the wrong number. I asked for Charlotte.

"Not here."

"Is this the right number?"

"Yes. Who is this?"

I thought it was Jimmy Korvos, but he sounded so harsh and angry, I couldn't be sure. "Mr. Korvos?"

Silence. Then he said, "Who is this?"

"This is Charlotte's sister."

"Oh." His voice changed a little. "Well, I don't know where the hell she is. If you catch up with her, tell her I want to see her, pronto." He hung up.

I was frightened, though I wasn't sure why. He had sounded so angry.

"What is it?" Marty said. "You're shaking."

I told him.

"Well, honey, don't worry till there's something to worry about. He may be mad because she wasn't there when he wanted her to be. Who knows?" He put his arm around me. "First rule for conquering depression: sufficient unto the day are the problems thereof. AA has the right idea, you know: don't borrow trouble."

He was right, and I tried to get it off my mind, but I couldn't. It was the drug thing that scared me. If Korvos had found out she was dealing and not giving him a cut . . . Or if other people had found out . . .

After I went to bed, I couldn't sleep. I put on my robe and went out by the pool, and pretty soon Marty came out too. He brought a bottle of Courvoisier, and we sat there holding hands, mostly in silence, sipping the cognac and looking at the stars. There was a cool breeze that made the water in the pool splash gently against the sides.

Finally I said, "I'm going to look for a room when I get back. I can't live off the Fleeters any longer. It's bothered me all along, and now I really can't do it anymore. I hope they won't be upset."

"Where will you go?"

"I don't know."

"Uh . . . you haven't seen my apartment yet but it's kind of nice. I could use a roommate." He held up his hand before I could answer. "There's one bedroom and a studio couch, and I swear I'll sleep on the couch and make no move till you're ready. I promise."

"It's not that. But I'd just be *your* charity case then, instead of the Fleeters'."

"Charity case! Look, lady, I've got designs on you that the Fleeters, I hope, never dreamed of. I want to spend the rest of my life with you."

"You do?" I don't know why I was so astonished, but I was.

"Yes, ma'am. I happen to be in love with you."

I held his hand tight. "Marty, I guess I feel the same."

"You guess."

"No, not guess. I do. But I still have to be on my own now. I have to prove something."

"I could let you pay half the rent."

"I could never afford that. I'll find a room somewhere. if not in Westwood, then in West Hollywood or somewhere . . ."

He interrupted. "You're not going to live in any West Hollywood fleabag. You'd get mugged first thing."

"Sufficient unto the day . . ."

"All right. Touché." He was silent a minute. "Would it make a difference if we got married?"

I tried to picture the fact that I was being proposed to by a movie star's son beside a swimming pool in La Jolla, but all I could really think about was how touched I was that he would ask me, when I was sure he would rather not be married at this time in his life. I said, "No, but I thank you. And if you'll please move over, I want to sit beside you." I squeezed in beside him in his chair, and we sat there a long time.

"One of the things I have to get straightened out in my head," I said finally, "is how I feel about sex. I can't seem to sort out what I really feel from what I've been told to feel."

He had his face against my neck, and it was hard to hear what he said. "My theory is there are two ways to spell Sex. One is S-E-X. The other is L-O-V-E."

"It sounds like a Rolaids commercial," I said.

He kissed me. "Love is good for you."

21 ❊ ❊

WE went back to Los Angeles sooner than we had intended, because I was still so uneasy about Charlotte. As soon as I got home, I started calling her again, but I couldn't reach her. The phone just rang and rang.

I tried to get my mind off it. I cooked dinner for Marty, and opened my mail. I had Christmas cards from some of the kids at home, and there was a card from Harvey that he had made himself. It said "Merry Christmas, Sissy," but it looked more like a Valentine, with two lopsided hearts joined together with a crooked arrow. It almost made me cry. There was a check for twenty dollars from Mom and Dad, and a short letter.

> Dear Sissy,
> We were sorry you couldn't come for the holidays, but naturally if you have a job, you couldn't leave. As your father says, it costs so much to travel now. Harvey misses you very much. I gave him a ukelele for Christmas and right away he learned some chords, and even plays melodies on one string. He has a real gift for music. Meg and Gert and Brenda all asked for your address. All are well. I understand the Fleeters are in Mexico. Must be nice to have money to throw around. I never hear a word from Charlotte.
> Love, Mother.

I had already had small presents from my three sisters. It was a long time since we had all been together for Christmas. For a few minutes I felt really homesick, not so much to be home now but to be there in the old days, before Robert died and the others went away, when Charlotte was still in high school and everybody loved her.

"My sister Charlotte was voted most likely to succeed in her class," I said. "In the year book it said, 'One of the new Beautiful People.'"

"And that's what she's after, I suppose."

"I guess so. Isn't that a strange thing to want?"

"It seems so to me. But to each his own."

He had bought a *Times* on the way home, and I picked up part of it, trying to get my mind off Charlotte. In the entertainment section there was a picture of Michael Barski, and a story about his company opening in San Francisco. I looked at the picture and wondered why I had ever been in such a dither about him.

The phone rang, and I leaped up. It was Charlotte.

"Sissy?"

"Charlotte! Where have you been? I've tried and tried to call you."

Her voice sounded strange. "Sissy, I'm in a bit of a jam. I need your help."

"What is it?" My stomach felt tight.

"I want you to go to the Ambassador Hotel and take a room for two. Make up a name, don't use your own. Call yourself Anne Smith. Anne Smith. Got it?"

"Yes, but why . . ."

"Listen. Take a bag, so you won't have to pay in advance. Go up to the room and wait for me."

"But what's happening?"

"Just do it, Sis, will you?"

"Of course."

"See you shortly." She rung off.

126

I told Marty and he frowned.

"Damn, I don't like that. You could get hurt. If it's a mess about the drug pushing, I mean those guys don't fool around, Syl."

"I'll be all right." I was already throwing a few things into a bag. I was frightened for Charlotte, but I felt better now that I had heard from her and could do something. "Marty, will you call me a cab?"

"Of course not. I'll take you down there. And listen, Syl, I'm going to take a room too. I'm going to be on hand if you need any help."

"That's silly, Marty. Really. I'll be all right."

"Maybe so, but I'm going to stick around."

We argued about it on the way down, but he wouldn't give up. He went in and registered first, so he could give me his room number. Then he got into the elevator and disappeared while I was registering.

I went up to the room they gave me and waited. It was a nice room; the Ambassador is a beautiful old hotel with acres and acres of gardens, but I was too nervous to enjoy any of it.

It seemed a very long time before there as a knock at the door, and then I half-expected it would be Marty. But it was Charlotte. She had a big shoulder bag but no suitcase. She was smiling in a way I remembered, a kind of defiant grin that she used to have when she had disobeyed Mom. It made me angry, probably just the way it did Mom. Here I'd been, worrying my heart out, and she sailed into the room as if nothing were wrong.

"Hi, Sis. Why are you looking so mad?"

"Charlotte. For heaven's sake. You call me up and give me all these mysterious instructions, fake name and all, and then you breeze in here and say why am I looking mad. I'm not mad, I've been *worried*. All right?"

"I'm sorry." She sat down on the bed. "Really I am, Sis.

Maybe I shouldn't have called you, but it was the only way I could think of to, you know, disappear."

"Why do you have to disappear?"

She didn't answer for a minute. She took off the floppy wide-brimmed hat, the kind she always liked to wear, and combed out her hair, and inspected her face in the mirror in her purse. "I look like hell."

"Charlotte, what is going on?" I had never taken this tone with her before in my life, and I saw the look of surprise that crossed her face. In the past if she upset me, I would go away, go to my room or for a walk or something, and never say anything. Now I was sounding as if I were the older one.

She took a deep breath. "It's not a charming story. You remember the other night I mentioned I was pushing drugs." As if she expected me to lecture her, she said, "And I was making real money, Sissy, big money. In a year I could have quit and been way ahead."

"So what happened?"

"Honey, I'm telling you. Don't rush me. It's not . . ." She paused for a minute, as if it were hard to go on, and I realized she was more upset than she had seemed. "It's not the easiest thing to explain." She took a deep breath, and got a cigarette from her purse. When she had lighted it, she said, "It seems I was doing too well. Some unpleasant types thought I was getting in their way. I was threatened."

"How threatened?"

"Well, I think the phrase was 'We're going to get you.' " She tried to laugh. "Right out of TV, isn't it?"

"My God, Charlotte." I felt as if I'd been kicked in the stomach.

" 'Your God' is right. Let us hope he comes to the rescue, the God of our fathers, Daddy's famous God. I could use a little divine interference."

"Is it Korvos that's after you?"

"Oh, no. He found out about it, and he's mad as a wet hen because I was making so much nice money for him and now it's spoiled. But he isn't about to kill me, not Jimmy."

"Kill you." I went and stood at the window, trying to get myself together. I told her about calling and getting Korvos on the phone.

"Well, he's no real threat. Beating me up is his idea of revenge. He's not about to kill the golden goose."

"What are you going to do?"

"I'm not sure. I want time to think. That's why I asked you to get me in here. I thought if I wasn't the one who registered, I wouldn't be remembered. I used the phone to get the room number for Anne Smith." Suddenly she giggled. "It's like when we were kids, making up fake names and playing parts."

Who but Charlotte would think of kids' games, when her life was in danger? She exasperated me beyond words, and I felt as protective as a mother hen.

"You don't have to stick around if you don't want to, Sissy. I'll be all right now."

"I'll stick around." I knew Marty would want me to clear out. He'd say I had done what I could and there was no sense risking my neck. But I couldn't do that. Charlotte was my sister; I loved her.

"Okay. It'll be a lot pleasanter. Why don't you ask room service to bring up some chicken sandwiches and a bottle of gin and some tonic water. I haven't eaten in quite a while."

She went into the bathroom when the room service cart came, so the waiter didn't see her.

"There," she said, pouring out a slug of gin. "I live again. Want some?"

"No, thanks. Don't drink too much, Charl. You'll need to be able to think."

"Don't preach, baby. I know what I'm doing."

If you did, I thought, you wouldn't be here, but I didn't say it. She turned on the TV and watched the Johnny Carson show. I was trying hard to think of what she could do. It all seemed so vague. Who were the people that threatened her? How serious was it? I asked her, but her answers were not very enlightening. I wasn't sure she really knew herself. I wondered if I should talk to Marty. Poor Marty, sitting in a room worrying.

"Are they Mafia?"

"Probably. I don't know."

I shivered. If all you hear about the mobs is true, it wasn't pleasant to think about. And I wished Charlotte would stop with the gin.

When Johnny Carson was over, Charlotte got a big manila envelope out of her bag and gave it to me. "I might have to go out of the country for a while. I went to a lawyer today and got a few things straightened out. It's all self-explanatory, no need to go over it now, but if I should have to leave in a hurry, you'll have it."

I put it in my bag.

She asked me if I had heard from Mom, and I told her what the letter had said.

"Harvey ought to have a piano," she said. "I've been saying that for years, but she always says it's too expensive. A ukelele, for Christ's sake! That's ludicrous."

"Well, don't waste energy getting mad at Mom now."

"No." She took off her clothes and got under the covers in one of the beds. "I tried to go back to the apartment after I saw the lawyer, but it was being watched. Damn it all, I haven't got a stitch. And worse than that, I've got a big bundle of cash stashed away in a shoebox in my closet. I'm going to need that cash." She was quiet for a minute. "Sissy, do you suppose . . ." Then she looked at me and said, "No, I guess not."

I was shocked. She had considered sending me back there,

risking my neck, for her damned money. She had changed her mind, but she *thought* of it.

"Oh, well," she said, "I'll get some clothes down here in the arcade. I can use my Diners."

"What will you pay for them with? I mean credit cards don't *give* you stuff."

"How true. But by the time the bills come — " She stopped and laughed. "They won't be able to find me."

I thought of Marty's "sufficient unto the day . . ." and again I wished that I could talk to him. But if Charlotte knew I had told him about her, she would feel betrayed.

"I ought to get out of the country." She was talking half to herself. "It would be the safest thing. But I don't have a passport. I've been meaning to get one, just in case, but I hadn't gotten around to it."

"You could get one tomorrow."

"They might be expecting me to do that. They might be watching. Anyway, tomorrow is New Year's Eve."

I realized with surprise that it was. The past week had seemed so unreal, I'd lost track of time.

She had another gin and tonic. I suppose it helped her nerves, but it didn't do much for mine. I was afraid she'd get smashed and do something reckless.

We watched the late evening news. I couldn't have told you anything they said.

There was a loud knock at the door. Charlotte was out of bed and into the bathroom before I could move. I tried to smoothe out her bed. The knock came again. I opened the door a crack and looked out, ready to slam it shut again if I had to.

A strange man stood there staring at me. As I started to shut the door, he said, "Wait, wait," and grabbed it. I pushed. "Hey, miss, don't do that. You'll mash my fingers."

He didn't sound like the Mafia. "What do you want?"

"I want old Freddie. Where's Freddie?"

He seemed drunk, but it could be an act. "I don't know any Freddie. You've got the wrong room." I shoved the door tight shut and locked all the locks. I could hear him still talking, but then it was quiet. "You can come out," I said to Charlotte.

She came out looking scared. "Jesus! That shook me up. Who was it?"

I told her.

She frowned "It could have been an act."

"It could."

"If anybody knocks again, no matter what, don't answer it." She scrunched down under the blankets.

"I think you ought to get out of here as soon as you can, Charlotte."

"Where am I going to go?"

I thought. Suddenly I had an idea. "I have a friend whose family live in Hawaii. I could find out from Shelley where you could stay and all that."

"Hawaii." She thought about it. Slowly she smiled. "Tropical paradise. No passport required. Away from the mainland. Sissy, I think you've got it."

"She lives in Hilo. . . ."

"No, not Hilo for me. It rains all the time. No action." She sat up, thinking. "But Honolulu . . . Maui? No, a lot of people go to Maui now, but there's no big center like Honolulu. I could stay at the Royal Hawaiian. It's old but it's got the ambience, and that's what I'll need."

"Have you been to Hawaii?"

"No, but honey, I read travel literature like other people read mystery stories."

"What about money?"

"I'm thinking." She hunched up her shoulders. She looked cold. I tossed her my bathrobe and she put it on.

"Shall I turn down the air conditioning?"

She shook her head, and got up to put more ice in her glass. She was drinking gin on the rocks now. "I can't use

132

my credit cards, because I'd have to fly under my own name. I don't want anyone tracing me."

"Is all your money in the shoebox?"

"Oh, God, no. That's just the take for the last few days. I haven't had time to go to the bank. I've got a savings account. Listen, in that manila envelope I gave you, among other things there's a power of attorney made out to you that covers my bank account. What you do is, draw out maybe five thousand, turn it into a cashier's check.... No, that won't do. I'd have to identify myself to cash it.... Let's see. Have them give you a cashier's check, five thousand, and turn it into cash in your own bank. Then bring me the cash at the airport. I hate to carry that much, but it's the only way I can think of."

It seemed unnecessarily complicated, but I had practically no knowledge of banks. They make me very nervous. I have a tiny account in the Westwood branch of Bank of America, but I only go there when I have to. "You'd better write it down, what I do. I'm not good at finance."

She found a memo pad and wrote it down. "Now. Airline reservation." She found the number in the phone book and dialed. While the number was ringing, she said, I need a name. Quick. Uh... Cathy for *Wuthering Heights* ... Leigh for Vivian Leigh.... Hello? I'd like to get a reservation for Honolulu for tomorrow. Do you have an evening flight ... Oh. Not till the first. Well, all right then ... First class, please. Can I pick it up at the airport? ... Fine." She was using a phony voice, deep and drawly with lots of broad *a*'s. "No, I'll pay cash.... Cathy Leigh, L-e-i-g-h. The Ambassador Hotel, room 412 ... Fine. Thank you so much." She hung up and threw up her arms in triumph. "I'm in business!"

I wished she hadn't used that expression. It was just as well she wasn't going to meet the Tanakas. They would probably be hospitable enough to keep track of her, and that could be disaster.

133

"You ought to lie low over there, though, shouldn't you, Charlotte? Just in case anybody's checking up?"

"Oh, at first, sure." She poured herself more gin. Her face was getting flushed. "Then I'll emerge, as if from . . . that's it, from mourning. The charming young widow, Cathy Leigh, Mrs. Charles Leigh, whose husband was so tragically killed in the crash of his private plane. He was . . . with the State Department, a very hush-hush job. When we weren't living in Washington, our home was in Northampton." She wrinkled her brow. "No, I never lived in Washington. Can't chance that. Northampton. A young widow in need of consolation."

"Charlotte, don't." The fact that it sounded like one of the games we used to play long ago made it all the harder to bear. This was real.

"Don't what? Fantasize? Darling, it's the way I make my living. I am always somebody else when the johns come knocking on my door. It's better than a play, and the cast of characters would astound you." She was all revved up now.

"You're going to have a hangover."

"Never have 'em." She slipped out of bed. "But I *am* going to take a shower. Damn, I wish I had some clothes, and that shoebox." She took her glass with her into the bathroom.

As soon as I heard the shower running, I dialed Marty's room. He answered on the first ring. "I'm all right. I'll be leaving in the morning."

"Thank God you called. Call me from the desk when you're ready. You'll be alone?"

"Yes."

"All right. Don't answer your door if anyone knocks. God, I've been sitting here dreaming up scenarios that would put John D. MacDonald to shame. Thanks for calling, love. I love you."

134

"Me too. Goodnight."

She was singing in the shower. When she came out, she got into bed beside me and put out the light. "I'm getting sleepy."

"Good. You should have some sleep."

She giggled. "You never used to sound so much like a mother."

"I'm older," I said. "About ten thousand years."

"Poor Sissy. You worry too much. *Que sera sera.*" She ran her fingers along the hem of the sheet. "Remember those awful sheets Mom always had? Muslin seconds, bought at the White Sales, and mended till they had bumps all over them?"

"Of course I remember. She still has them."

"Don't sound so cross." She snuggled against me, and for a moment I thought of all those men, and I had to fight the impulse to pull away. I guess my feelings toward my sister at that time — maybe all the time now — could be called ambivalent. I thought of my psych professor. It seemed so long since I had been in classes.

"I'm never going to have anything but satin sheets ever in my lifetime. I've tasted luxury and it's just as delicious as I dreamed it would be. Satin sheets, Irish linen tablecloths, sterling silver. A full-length mink coat, Sissy. How does that grab you? Would I look sensational in a full length Blackglama? Living legend?"

"You'd look sensational all right, but living legends have to do something to become one, don't they?"

"Don't be silly. Is Zsa Zsa Gabor the world's greatest actress? Was the Duchess of Windsor some kind of talent? Image, darling, image is the name of the game." Her voice was getting drowsier. "Sissy, dear Sissy, you are so good to me. Forgive me for slapping you. It was a terrible thing to do."

"That's all right."

"You had hurt me, that's why I reacted."

"I'm sorry, Charlotte. I was upset too."

"I know. Moment of truth. But now you know, and you've grown up and accepted it. But those ugly words you used, that's not me. Think of the great courtesans of history, honey. Nobody bad-mouths Lady Hamilton. Nobody sneers at Josephine."

"Josephine married Napoleon."

"But she didn't marry all those other chaps. Some day you'll be proud of me, Sissy dear. You'll say, 'That's my glamorous sister, that lady there having caviar for breakfast. . . .' " Her voice trailed off and she fell asleep.

I stroked her hair with the tips of my fingers, stroked that expensive casual hairdo. Charlotte, my sister, sleeping like a child, dreaming of mink and caviar.

22 ❋ ❋

O N the rainy morning of New Year's Eve Marty drove me first to Charlotte's lawyer's office in Beverly Hills. She had remembered to tell me I had to get my signature witnessed on the power of attorney. I was afraid the lawyer would ask questions, but I didn't even see him. His secretary witnessed the signature and notarized it.

At the bank Marty went in with me and explained to an assistant manager what I wanted. No problem. The young man was gone a few minutes, and came back with a cashier's check for five thousand dollars made out to me. It was a very weird experience to have that thing in my purse.

It was even weirder after we had been to my bank and I had all that money. Marty didn't like my having it with me. We decided I would spend the night at his place, and then we switched the plan to my place in case Charlotte needed to get in touch with me.

"I'll be glad when she's gone," he said. "I don't like it one bit. It puts you at risk."

I would be glad when she was safely gone too, but mostly on her account. I didn't feel concerned about myself except that some New Year's Eve drunk might hit me over the head and take the cash. We decided to stay home and celebrate, if that was the word.

We stashed the money away in Maddie's electric teakettle, wrapping it first in a packet of waxed paper. I began to laugh, just a touch hysterically.

"What is it?"

"I was just thinking, if we were spirited away on a UFO tonight, and Maddie came home and started to make tea, how surprised she'd be." We both laughed a lot harder than the idea was worth.

Marty went down to the village and got some champagne and half a smoked turkey and some other stuff, and we ate in front of the TV, trying to pretend we weren't nervous.

The plan was that I should get to the airport and pick up the ticket and meet Charlotte at the place where they frisk you. Marty said he would go with me.

"I deserve one glimpse of the Magnificent Charlotte," he said.

I kept thinking how relieved I'd be on my parents' account to have her off the mainland. They'd never have any reason to find out about her in Hawaii. We didn't have the kind of friends that jetted over to Honolulu for the holidays or anything like that. Poor Mom, if she ever knew the truth.

That night when Marty came into my room to say goodnight, I pulled him down to the bed. "Let's make love." I heard the little gasp he gave.

"Syl, are you sure?"

"Yes, I'm sure."

He was very gentle, and I felt a kind of happiness I had no idea existed. Outside, horns blew and people yelled and sirens went off.

"The whole world knows," Marty said softly in my ear. "Happy new year, darling."

We had to get up a lot sooner than we wanted to, to meet Charlotte at the airport. It was still raining, but the world looked fine to me. We stopped at Marty's place while he ran in for something or other. It was the first time I had even seen it from the outside, and I liked it very much. It was a small apartment house on a cul-de-sac. He was back in a few minutes wearing his raincoat. I teased him about being afraid of a little California dew.

It was new to me to have a relationship like this, where I felt so close to somebody, so relaxed and warm, as if Marty were another part of myself that I hadn't known existed, and yet he wasn't me, he was separate and complete in himself, and I was separate and complete in myself. It was hard to put into words in my mind, but the feeling was very strong and real and good. When I had felt sick and miserable, he had been there to look after me, but he didn't try to dominate. He knew when to let me be. I felt so happy.

When we got to the airport and were looking for the departure area, I was thinking that somehow loving Marty made me feel different toward Charlotte too. I still loved her, but she wasn't my idol anymore; she was my sister, and she was in bad trouble, and I was going to help her. I could see her as a human being. In a way I think I loved her more.

We walked down the long corridors, me clutching the ticket and the packet of money in both hands, I was so afraid somebody would snatch them.

Charlotte wasn't there, but we were a little early. The closed-circuit schedule listed the plane as leaving on time. We found a bench and sat down to wait.

Marty kept glancing at the other passengers, trying to spot anybody who looked suspicious. They looked perfectly normal. Families off to Hawaii for a vacation, businessmen on a trip, the usual thing. Neither of us could find much to talk about at that point.

The time for Charlotte's arrival came, and went. "She's always late," I said. My hand that held the flat package of money and the ticket was clammy. I couldn't sit still; I kept crossing and recrossing my legs. Marty went to a vending

139

machine and brought back two cups of dreadful coffee. We drank it and made faces at each other.

"If she tried to reach me and we had already left ... ," I said.

"She would have called here and had you paged." He went over to one of the airline people to make sure we hadn't missed a call for me, in all the announcements constantly being made on the p.a. He came back, shaking his head.

The minutes on the abominable clock in front of us ticked past. I went to a phone and called the room I had had at the Ambassador.

They said the party had checked out. No message, but she left a forwarding address: Mrs. Charles Leigh, 49 Elm Avenue, Northampton, Mass. I told Marty what they said.

I was puzzled. Had she changed her plans, and was that supposed to be some kind of message for me? I couldn't read it. Then it came to me. "That's in case anybody comes looking for her at the hotel. In case anybody followed her there. There's nobody named Charlotte Duncan registered, just a Mrs. Leigh who lives in Massachusetts."

He widened his eyes. "When first we practice to deceive, what a damned bloody tangled web we weave."

"Charlotte's web."

He groaned. "Now we're into puns. Listen, how long do we wait?"

"Till the plane goes. She perfectly capable of streaking in here just as they're pulling up the gangplank or whatever."

"Not *streaking,* darling," he said, and then looked as if he was sorry he said it.

"Dashing. Whatever." I looked at the clock. The man at the check-in desk announced the flight, and people lined up to board. I walked out so I could see down the corridor. No Charlotte.

140

When the last passengers had gone through, we still waited. A late man with a briefcase darted past the attendant, waving his ticket. Then the attendant disappeared, came back in a few minutes, and closed the gate. Marty caught up with him and asked if the plane had gone.

"Yes, sir."

We waited a few more minutes and then went back to my place, not talking at all. I was really frightened, and trying hard to persuade myself she had changed her plans for some reason.

"She did check out, we know that," Marty said. "I think she had to change plans and went east."

"She didn't have any money."

"She might have risked using her credit card. I prophesy you'll hear that phone ring before evening."

"I hope so." I had a terrible feeling that we were whistling in the dark, but I didn't know what to do.

"Sylvia," Marty said, "this is terrible timing, but I have to tell you or I'll burst. I'm in love with you. I mean the real thing. I want to marry you. I don't want to let you out of my sight ever again, though I know that's not exactly a practical wish."

He took me so by surprise, I couldn't think of anything to say. It was hard to switch my mind from worry about Charlotte to being proposed to.

He looked anxious. "I should have waited till you weren't worried about Charlotte."

"Marty." For some reason I began to cry, and I didn't know whether it was about Charlotte or about Marty.

He put his arms around me. "Don't cry."

"I'm sorry. It's been such a day. Such a week. I do love you, Marty."

He kissed me.

"But wait a while, all right? I can't seem to think straight."

"I know. I should have kept my big mouth shut."

"No, you shouldn't. I'm just not reacting right. I'm mixed up."

"I know. It's okay. Don't worry about it."

We sat quietly with our arms around each other. An odd thought went through my mind: this was going to be the biggest decision of my life so far, and I was going to make it entirely by myself. No advice from anyone, no instructions, no help.

Suddenly the doorbell rang, loud and demanding, and I was on my feet before it stopped. I knew something had happened to Charlotte, and I was trembling with fear.

Marty opened the door, and there was a strange man in a rumpled raincoat. For a moment I thought he was somebody from the Mafia, looking for my sister. But he held out a badge, and my heart began to thump in hard, painful thumps.

"I'm Perelli, from Robbery-Homicide." He was an ordinary-looking man, not official-looking, more like a postman or a door-to-door salesman. He had a soft, almost apologetic voice. "Are you Sylvia Duncan?"

"What is the matter?" He had said Robbery, and for a second I thought maybe she was accused of stealing something, but that didn't make sense. He had said Robbery-Homicide. I wanted to run. If I didn't hear what he had to say, it wouldn't have happened. But I couldn't move.

He glanced at Marty, and Marty said, "I'm her fiancé. I'll stay, if it's all right."

"Sure. Mind if I take off my coat? Wet outside. Darned L.A. rain, it never quits."

Marty took his coat. It was like a cocktail party or something. What had happened to Charlotte? I thought I had asked him, but then I realized I hadn't said anything. I tried again, and my voice came out sounding strangled. "What has happened to my sister?" I felt as if I were balancing on an edge, with a long drop below me.

He cleared his throat, and his Adam's apple moved up and down. "Miss Duncan, I have bad news."

"I *know* that. What is it?" I wanted to grab him and shake him. How could he take so long?

"She was attacked."

I felt sick to my stomach. "How badly is she hurt?"

"I'm sorry. She's dead."

"No." My voice was calm now. It seemed necessary to correct this crazy mistake he had made. Of course Charlotte was not dead. Anything else might have happened; she might be hurt, she might have been arrested, but she couldn't be dead. She had never planned for that.

Marty took my arm and led me to the sofa.

"I'm real sorry," the officer said.

Marty said, "What happened?"

"She was stabbed with a thin knife in the back."

I heard the sound I made. I thought someone else had made it.

"She must have died before she hardly knew she was hit. It was one straight stab into the heart. Almost no blood."

"Almost no blood," I said. I was glad there had been almost no blood. Blood always made Charlotte feel sick. Once when Harvey cut his head open, she fainted.

Marty brought me some brandy, but I didn't touch it. Why do they bring you liquor when everything is smashing up all around you?

"Where was she?" Marty asked.

"In the parking area behind her apartment house. She had a suitcase that was broken open, clothes scattered. Hard to tell if anything was stolen."

"Did she have a shoebox?" If she didn't have the shoebox, it wasn't Charlotte. Somebody else, somebody else. They had made a mistake.

"Yes, there was an empty shoebox."

I wanted to hit him. I felt suddenly furious, angry with

Charlotte, too, for being so stupid. She knew she should not go back there. Just for a few clothes and some money she didn't even need.

He asked some questions, when had I last seen her, when had we talked. Like an Agatha Christie book. Not real.

"Would you like me to tell him?" Marty said. "About Charlotte?"

"No, of course not." She wasn't his sister, she was mine. I told him everything I knew. I hated telling him.

He left finally. Marty saw him out. I sat there trying to get it through my head. Charlotte was dead, truly dead. But I didn't really believe it even yet. I couldn't cry. I just kept saying over and over in my mind, "Listen. Charlotte is dead."

23 ❀ ❀

THEY asked me to identify the body. Marty tried to protest, but I went when they told me the alternative was to fly my parents in. Somebody had to do it. Marty went with me, down the long cold corridors of the police morgue, but I asked him to wait while I went up to that white-sheeted figure and looked at my sister. I had to do it alone.

It was Charlotte, and it wasn't Charlotte. Of course it was, technically, and she didn't look as if anything violent had happened to her. But it was like a statue of Charlotte, all the life and laughter and vivacity gone. I nodded to the policeman, and found the ladies' room and vomited.

I don't remember going home. There was one more thing I had to do; I had to call my mother. The police had offered to do it, but that would have been too terrible.

When I got my mother on the phone, I told her that Charlotte had been killed by an unknown person, outside her apartment house. I heard her catch a breath and then I knew she was crying. She said, "This will kill your father."

I wanted to comfort her, but I couldn't think what to say.

Finally she said, "I'll come out.

I told her I would make a plane reservation for her and call her back. I did that, and then I fell apart. Marty held

145

me and I cried and cried and cried. I tried to tell him what a waste it had been, how senseless it was.

Lieutenant Perelli was back the next day, apologizing for bothering me. He was a kind man. He asked some more questions about Jimmy Korvos, and I told him all I knew. They had picked him up when he came back to the apartment looking for Charlotte. Apparently he had an albi.

"Miss Duncan, do you know if she left a will?"

I got the manila envelope and Perelli spread the papers out on the coffee table. There was a carbon copy of a will, the original at the lawyer's office, it said. He asked me to look at it. She had left everything to me except for twenty-five hundred dollars to buy a piano and music lessons for Harvey.

There was the power of attorney, which I had slipped back in the envelope after I finished with it. There was her savings bank book with a balance of twenty one thousand, two hundred dollars. There was a life insurance policy payable to me, twenty thousand dollars.

"My God!" Marty said.

Lieutenant Perelli was looking at a small piece of monogrammed stationery. "Ah!" he said with satisfaction.

"What is it?"

He read it to us. "If anything happens to me, tell the cops to check up on Cyril Evans." He looked up at us. "Cyril Evans. She was poaching on dangerous ground. Evans is a very busy boy in the drug world." He stood up. "I'd like to get all these things photocopied, Miss Duncan. I'll get them back to you. The autopsy is finished. When your mother gets here, she can claim the body anytime."

Claim the body. Claim Charlotte. I hated him for speaking of her as "the body." But I said, "My mother will be here tonight."

After he was gone, I looked at Marty and saw how pale he looked. "Poor Marty. You didn't know what you were getting into. If you want to clear out, it's all right."

He shook his head as if I exasperated him. "Don't talk nonsense. Look, will you take a Valium and get some sleep?" I didn't take the Valium but I lay down for a while.

My mother looked twenty years older. Her face was like something carved out of ivory. Marty and I met her at the airport, but I don't think she was really aware of Marty at all for a long time. She asked only practical questions. She wanted Charlotte buried in Los Angeles, because she thought it would be easier on my father and Harvey. "Harvey needn't know anything about it, if it's done out here," she said in a tone that sounded as if she expected me to argue with her. "I won't have him suffering."

Marty helped her find a mortuary and all that. I chose the casket. My mother and Marty thought it should be an inexpensive one.

"They rip you off," Marty said.

But I insisted on one that looked luxurious and had blue satin lining. "She loved satin sheets," I said. They didn't argue with me anymore.

We buried my sister in the Valley. My mother stood by the open grave a long time, silent tears streaming down her face. "She was the one most like me," she said to no one in particular. "She was the one I loved."

That night when we were alone, she talked about Meg and my other two sisters and the grandchildren, about my father's parishioners, about everything but Charlotte, and every once in a while she would give a terrible, strangling sob. But in a minute she would go on talking again, as if it hadn't happened. There was no way I could reach her.

She called my father on the phone, but I didn't hear what she said. "He is in shock," she said afterward. "I talked to Meg."

I said, "Mom, you haven't asked me anything about Charlotte's life or how she died."

"I know how she died. Some criminal murdered her. I don't want to know any more."

"But these things get in the papers." There had been a short item in the *Times* about the murder, not identifying her as a call girl, but if some inquisitive reporter chased it down, there could be all kinds of hell. A murdered hooker is a story they love.

"I shall not read it if there is. And no one will mention it to me."

Looking at her face, I knew she was right, no one would mention it to her.

"I'll send you the check for Harvey's piano."

"They cost a lot."

"But Charlotte left the money in the will. She loved Harvey."

Her face twisted for a moment, and she turned away from me.

While she was packing, I put the rest of the five thousand dollars in her purse. If I mentioned it, she would refuse it, but if she found it after she had gone, an accomplished fact, I thought she would keep it. I wished I knew how to give her something more than money. I would love her if she would let me. I would offer her comfort. I knew how she suffered, because I was suffering, too. But she was too far away for me to get to. That night after I had gone to bed, I lay awake and wept for a long time, thinking how alone we all are.

24 ❋❋

MADDIE came back two days later. She was terribly shocked to hear about Charlotte, but I don't think it seemed very real to her. She had had a wonderful time in Mexico, mainly because Donnie had come down and her parents approved of him. They were talking about getting married in June. I told her that I would be moving out. She seemed almost relieved, and I realized that Donnie was probably longing to move in.

"Where are you going to live, Sissy?"

"There's an apartment a block from where Marty lives. Unfurnished, so I can do it the way I want to."

"Why a block away? I mean that nice Marty Ross — what are you waiting for?"

"I have to be alone for a while." I had tried to explain it to Marty, and I think he understood. I needed time to take in all that had happened to me. I guess I would have changed a lot that first year away from home anyway, but what had happened to Charlotte and then my falling in love with Marty had sprung it on me almost overnight. I had to sort it out and see where I stood. I was pretty sure I would marry Marty someday, but first I needed to do a lot of thinking, about my education, my plans for my life, my values.

Marty picked me up that afternoon and drove me downtown to look for furniture for my apartment. I wanted to get settled as quickly as possible. We had dinner afterward at the Biltmore.

My sister Charlotte had been dead exactly one week. Most of the time it still wasn't believable to me. All that warmth and affection, all that perversity and self-destruction, the love of beautiful things, the amorality, the make-believe, all of it Charlotte. It seemed so sad that she couldn't have found someone she could let herself love. It made such a difference. In my mind I could hear her saying, "That's *your* cup of tea, Sis. It isn't necessarily mine." But her cup of tea had killed her. Maybe a person can't ever make head or tail of someone else's life, or for that matter of their own, but I had to try, without anybody looking over my shoulder, without any road maps drawn up by someone else, without sermons.

The next day I got a very warm, nice letter from Mrs. Fleeter about Charlotte. She said, "The whole town is shocked. Charlotte was always so popular. I went to see your mother this afternoon. She is holding up beautifully. Poor Harvey has not been told. Your mother says he won't remember even after he knows. If there is anything we can do to help in any way, Sissy, please let me know. We so appreciate what you have done for us, making it possible for Maddie to adjust so well. We were delighted with her young man. You are a sane, strong girl, Sissy, and a help to us all. Affectionately, Jennifer Fleeter."

I thought about Mrs. Fleeter quite a while, and then I told Maddie I would have to write her and tell her I was moving out and try to explain why

Maddie didn't want me to do it. "Why not just let it ride till summer? By then it will be a fait accompli, and she'll take it in her stride. Now she is apt to get all nervous again and make me live in a dorm or something. I couldn't *stand* that. Donnie and I have got to have a place of our own."

I thought about it some more. I hated to do that to Maddie, but I couldn't just sneak out, after all the Fleeters had done for me. I had resented having things done for me, because I'm a feisty person who spent too many years being done for, but nevertheless the Fleeters had meant to be kind and generous. Without their help I might never have met Marty.

Maddie still tried to talk me out of it. "Ask Marty. I bet he'll side with me."

"It doesn't make any difference whether he does or not."

She looked so shocked, I tried to explain. "I mean, I love Marty, but he can't do my thinking for me."

In the end I decided to call Mrs. Fleeter up. It scared me to death; I've never liked telephones. But it seemed as if I might be able to explain things better.

I hadn't made many long-distance calls, and I was startled at how quickly she was on the phone, sounding as close as if she were in the room.

I did some stumbling around but finally I got it said. She was silent for a few seconds, and I was afraid I had really blown it for Maddie.

Then she said, "Thank you for calling me, Sissy. Of course I see your point. I guess there comes a time for all of us when we have to go it alone. And if you are all right financially . . ."

"Yes, I am now, but it isn't that. I mean I had been thinking about this anyway. I love living with Maddie, I really do, but I just have to see if I can hack it on my own."

"Oh, you'll hack it all right. No question there. All you ever had to do was to reach the point where you knew your own strength." She gave a little laugh, and said, "I suppose when you move out, Donnie will move in, before the door even closes."

What could I say? "They really love each other, Mrs. Fleeter," I said finally, when the pause was getting too long.

"Oh, I believe that. And that's what the young people do nowadays. I just have to realize that Maddie is grown up. Well, Sissy, I wish you all the luck in the world, my dear, and if you ever need us for anything, do let us know."

I thanked her a couple of times, and that was that. I called Maddie out of her room where she had fled when I phoned her mother, and I told her it was going to be all right. Then I went into my room and flopped on the bed and thought. The bridges were burned. Now, there were no alibis about parents holding me back, no Fleeters to prop me up, no Charlotte to look to. I was Sylvia.

25 ❀ ❀

THE day I moved into my new apartment was a happy one until late that afternoon. Marty had been helping me arrange the furniture and unpack and we were both tired. He opened a bottle of wine and we flopped on the new sofa, with packing stuff all around us and books piled up on the floor.

"Got something for you." He gave me a funny look, as if he were nervous.

"What is it?"

He reached into his jeans pocket and took out a blue ring box. He opened it up and thrust it at me.

The ring was a beautiful diamond set in a circle of small sapphires. I looked at him. "It's beautiful."

"It was my mother's engagement ring, from my father."

I felt scared.

"Put it on. Here, I will. It may be a bit big for you...."

I didn't put out my hand. Instead I got up and walked to the window and looked out. Somebody was parking a Lincoln Continental across the street. "Marty." My voice sounded far off.

"What's the matter?"

I knew I was upsetting him, and I didn't want to. "Marty, if I wear that ring, that means we're engaged. Formally. Almost like being married."

153

"It's nothing like being married." He sounded stiff, and I knew in a minute he'd be angry.

I turned around to look at him. "But it's a formal promise to be married. I'm not ready for that. I haven't even had my eighteenth birthday yet. You're only twenty, with years of college and interning and all, ahead of you."

"That's my worry." His mouth was tight, with little white lines at the corners. "Are you saying you want to be free to play the field? Is that what you're saying?"

I was getting angry myself. It wasn't fair to push me like this. "No, that's not what I mean. I love you and you know it. Someday we'll probably get married. . . ."

" 'Probably.' That's great. That makes me feel really terrific. All this time I thought you loved me. . . ."

"Damn it, I do love you. Be reasonable. I'm only a freshman in college. I don't even know for sure what I want to major in, let alone what I want to do with my life."

"Where did I get the impression you wanted to spend it with me?"

"Spending it with you doesn't mean I file myself away in a drawer that says 'Marty's Wife,' and never do anything for myself."

"You're selfish."

"All right, then I'm selfish. Until very recently I haven't had a chance to be. Maybe I'd like to try it out for a while. Oh, Marty, please listen. I don't want to fight with you. My God, you of all people!"

He shoved the ring box back into his pocket and grabbed his jacket. "Well, I'll see you around." He slammed the door as he went out.

I sat down on the floor, with my head against the sofa. All the joy of the day was gone. I wanted to run after him and say, "Anything you want. I do love you." Because I did love him. But I couldn't do it. It just wouldn't work. I couldn't ever be a person with an apostrophe any more, not

Robert's twin or Charlotte's sister or Mom's daughter. Not Marty's wife. Someday I'd like to get married, and as far as I could tell, Marty would be the one, but that time was a long way off, and anything could happen. The main thing was, I had to stand on my own feet.

But I felt terrible. I made myself get up and go on with the unpacking. It got to be six o'clock and then seven, but I didn't stop to eat. I felt too miserable.

At seven-twenty the doorbell rang. My heart leaped, but I thought it was probably Maddy. I smoothed back my hair and went to the door. At first all I could see was this absolutely enormous bunch of tea roses. Then Marty's face appeared, as he held the roses out to me.

"Are you going to let me in? These things won't keep if we don't put them in some water."

"Oh, Marty." I leaned past the flowers and kissed him.

He grinned, looking happy again, and came into the apartment. While we found a plastic bucket to put the roses in, he said, "Sylvia, thank you for letting me in. If I were you, I wouldn't have let in such a blithering dope, such a pushy, obtuse, bad-tempered bastard. . . ."

I kissed him to stop the names he was calling himself. "You do understand, then."

"I understand, but I hate it. And I warn you, I'll probably try to change your mind a million times. But of course I understand. You've got a right to be your own person, without feeling threatened."

"It will work better in the end. It's the *only* way it would work."

"And when we do get married, we don't want to be one of those three out of two California marriages that smash up. But you've got to understand me too. I mean, I had what you might call a kind of peculiar early life. I learned young not to count on anybody to be there when I needed them. When I began to realize how much I need you, well, it scared the hell out of me. I'll be jealous and possessive and hypersensitive and depressed from time to time, sometimes singly, sometimes all at once. Can you stand it?"

"We'll learn to stand each other."

He kissed me a long time. "All right, get your coat and let's get out of here. I'm starving."

I just looked at him a minute, and then we both laughed.

"I mean," he said, "how'd you like to go out to dinner?"

I said, "I'd love to."